INFINITE HERO

THE AWAKENING

Andy Bex

ISBN: 978-0-9956084-1-2

Table of Contents

The Prologue

It is a strange, wild and varied world upon which we live. But where ever you go, two and two will always make four and an action will always have an equal and opposite reaction. So no matter what size, colour or uniform we wear, people are people, wherever they come from.

The Loch

"Mr. Gregory, Duncan Gregory!"

Gregory, paused briefly, he thought about moving on, then changed his mind and turned to see who had called him. Gregory was lean but broad shouldered, handsome with thick brown hair, he wore slacks, comfortable boots and a tweed jacket, but had all the appearance of a wolf in nerd's clothing. It was dark and cold; Gregory's target was the local pub imaginatively called, "The Loch Inn." The warm light flooded through the windows and bathed the street. A large fan spread the unique smell of a British pub, warmth, beer, steak pie and a little smoke, that evoked compelling friendliness and the lost days of youth.

Gregory again looked round to the beckoning door of the pub and reluctantly answered, in perfect BBC English.

"Can I help you?"

The other man, skipped enthusiastically up to Gregory but stopped well out of arms reach, Gregory subconsciously noted this.

"Er, Yes, I am Ian Anderton, er, I'm a reporter."

Gregory, wasted no more time, he moved for the door, he wanted his pint and stated bluntly,

"There is a press conference tomorrow before the dive."

Gregory started to open the door, but Anderton foolishly lunged in and grabbed the handle.

"It's not about the dive, it's about you .... Sean Agostino!"

The two locked eyes, Anderton paled and swallowed hard. He knew he had overstepped the mark and if his suspicions were right, this was the last man he would want to offend.

Gregory smiled and shrugged. "OK, but you're buying the beers." He casually stepped to one side, imperceptible to the other man he lowered his elbow, which was about to crash into Anderton's cheek bone and retrieved his foot from behind Anderton's ankle.

The reporter was alive with expectation. He had rehearsed again and again how to deliver his lines, however, his focus distracted him from his surroundings. He clumsily bowled directly into a large bearded local, who was skilfully balancing three pints of beer between his hands. Anderton, knocked out the lead pint, crash and without the mutual support, the other two followed, crash, crash. Everyone in the pub turned, the large local looking at his beer-soaked feet.

"I'm er sorry, I'll buy you some more."

"You, Twat!"

"I'm sorry, it was an accident."

"I'll give you a fucking accident." The bearded man was a barrel-bellied 18 stone monster, two of his friends of equal stature stood up at the adjacent table, the owners of the other two pints. The man theatrically rolled up his sleeves and suddenly seemed to remember his collar was too small, strutting his neck out like a rooster.

"Hey, he said he was sorry." Forward stepped Gregory.

The large man started to laugh; his exaggerated movements were for his audience. "Oh, this is rich; the first ponce has a nerd to stick up for him. Aren't you one of this year's batch of Nessie hunters?"

No reply. Gregory just stood staring, eye to eye. This unsettled the big fellow; this is not how the game was played.

"Too scared to stick up for yourself?" then as an afterthought, "You little shit!"

Again no reply, just the eyes, but the message was clear: stick or bust; but before the cards were dealt, the landlord stepped in.

"McTaggish, I'll not have you starting trouble again, now out you go and take your mates with you." The big fellow, clearly wary of his opponent, grasped his moment to escape with honour and stormed out with his mates, full of abuse.

"Sorry, Mr. Gregory, he's not normally like that." the landlord lied.

"No problem Angus, can you set us up two pints of your best bitter and he's paying" Gregory shook his head at the ashen Anderton. The two moved up to the bar, Gregory put a pint glass down on the bar, this time Anderton did notice.

"So, who did you say I was?" said the relaxed Gregory.

"Er, I, er ", then remembering his lines, "Sean Agostino."

Gregory smiled, "Go on, give me your best…. Oh thanks Angus." Gregory paused, looked at the creamy swirling beer that Angus had just handed him, he seemed to meditate upon it and then he ritualistically rubbed his finger around the top, with the same care of that of the Japanese tea ceremony. He drank deep and gulped down a third of it. He licked his lips then wiped them with the back of his hand.

"Umm. Did you know they brew a pint in the States called 'The Loch Ness Monster' – have to try it someday, anyway what were you saying, ah yes, go on then, give me your best pitch."

This was not going as Anderton had rehearsed, but he launched into his speech anyway.

"Two years ago I covered the Agora incident for my paper. The man involved in that was a certain Sean Agostino, some said he was CIA, others FBI, others still SAS. I wanted to know more about this man, so I tracked him down. Two weeks later he was burned to death in a car crash!"

"How unfortunate, Mr. Anderton." Then another gulp of the beer.

"More, unfortunate than you can imagine, because he had already died in a car crash four years earlier." If Anderton had expected this revelation to get a response, then he was badly mistaken.

"Oh, what a shot!" Gregory was more focussed on the Premiership football highlights, on the large television in the corner of the bar.

Unperturbed Anderton continued, "So, Agostino lived a perfectly normal life as a software engineer, has a car crash and dies, then leaps up as an international Mr. fix it, speaking at least seven languages and with an arsenal of deadly skills."

Gregory turned and smiled broadly, "Well maybe he went to night school, did you think of that? You didn't, did you?" He winked.

Anderton pushed on, "And when I got near this man, he miraculously has another car crash and dies, with his body being burnt beyond recognition."

"It's an interesting story, Anderton, but what's it got to do with me?"

"Well imagine my surprise, Mr. Gregory, to find that same Sean Agostino masquerading as an acoustic's engineer on a seemingly trivial Nessie hunt on Loch Ness."

"What brought you here Anderton?" The slightest furrow creased Gregory's brow.

"Coincidence, I am on holiday with my family." Anderton noticed Gregory relax slightly, only very slightly.

"I don't believe in coincidence." He turned and grinned wickedly, moved his head next to Anderton's.

"So if I kill you now, who will know you've been here?" Gregory enjoyed the shock on Anderton's face, "Ah, but don't tell me you've mailed all your evidence to the police, damn!" Gregory shook his head in mock annoyance.

"For God's sake, Gregory, do you take anything seriously?"

"Well, not 'Your 'story anyway, you basically don't have anything do you?"

"Ah, you see I saved the best to last, I've checked up on you and guess what? Duncan Gregory also...." and then together in harmony with Gregory, "was killed in a car accident."

"OK, you've got my attention, what can I do for you?" says the still smiling Gregory.

"Well, I would not normally take any interest in the annual Nessie hunt, 'cause I think it's a load of bollocks, but if you're involved I think there might be something in it. I am hearing some interesting things from yesterday. Apparently, you fired an acoustic 'ping' at the Loch and you got back one almighty 'pong' in response. I am pretty sure that whatever you are looking for, it ain't Nessie."

Gregory downed the last of his pint, "OK, that's me; I'm walking back to the hotel. I'll tell you what; this is going to be a big story, but not now, not yet." He got up and made for the door, but Anderton rushed in front of him and stood with his back to the door.

"When then?"

"Soon. Why don't you join me on the boat tomorrow and you'll see?"

With that Anderton turned and walked out of the pub onto the street, but before his foot touched the floor, Gregory kicked him in the back and he flew headfirst into the road.

"What the fuck!" Anderton knew that he was dealing with a trained killer, but betrayal flamed his anger. He turned and was amazed to see McTaggish and his two friends crowded around the door. McTaggish was yelping and holding his hand, his punch aimed at Anderton had missed, thanks to Gregory and instead he had hit the door jamb. Like the precise movement of a robot building cars, Gregory moved through the three men. McTaggish went down with a twang as a side kick to the knee snapped his tendons. The man on the left collapsed holding his throat as a wicked rabbit punch smashed into his Adam's apple. The last flipped over doing a half back summersault as Gregory elbowed him in the face, but had somehow got one leg behind him to flip him over. The fight had lasted less than two seconds.

Gregory came over and calmly said,

"Up you get Anderton, so see you on the boat at 05:00. Don't be late." With that, he was away up the street.

The next morning Anderton arrived promptly for 05:00. He was pretty sure that he would be stood there alone, with Gregory either still lying in his bed or already well up the loch, laughing at him; but despite his fears the boat, the team and Gregory were all there waiting for him.

The boat sailed at 07:00 and sluggishly made its way several miles up the loch. By 8:30 the crew had started their search for Nessie. The scientists were in the close confines of the control room, it was dark, the room rocked gently, the 'fut fut' of the engines could be heard in the background and there was a noticeable smell of diesel.

Gregory stood behind the leader of the expedition, an extremely attractive forty-something female doctor in the field of acoustics, she was giving instructions to a man sat behind the console, guiding BOB the submersible.

Anderton whispered into Gregory's ear.

"You're not looking for Nessie are you?"

Gregory grinned, "They are!"

Anderton was aware that Gregory was standing well inside the personal space of the doctor and figured they must have something going on between them, interesting he thought, he wouldn't have thought that Gregory was the type to allow emotional baggage. He watched as Gregory put his hand on her shoulder, she turned around and smiled at Gregory. Her face was beautiful, almost flawless, she looked like a woman out of an anti-aging cream advert, clear olive skin, with only the slightest of laugh lines around her eyes, which were large and almond coloured. Her thick hair was rolled up and pinned by a wooden peg, simple but very effective. The only imperfection was her left eyelid, it was only slightly more closed than the other, but this minor imperfection itself was charming. Anderton could only think what a lucky man Gregory was.

The submersible had been descending for some time. A monitor on the table showed BOB's on-board camera, the depths of the loch were inky black, even with the large lights mounted on the sub.

"Nearly at the bottom Doctor."

Sure enough, as the operator spoke, dark shapes loomed into view showing the undulating bottom of the loch. Still, it was pretty dull, just more blackness, with fewer black shapes.

The doctor turned back to the operator and stated flatly,

"OK send the 'Ping' at 10% strength."

The operator had no big red button, just a mouse and a second monitor, he clicked on a button labelled 'Send' and immediately a rather satisfying low frequency 'bong' noise rattled from the ship, like in one of those black and white submarine movies. The noise could physically be felt not just heard and was immediately followed by a squeal of binary, like a fax machine. There was silence for a moment, then another noise, but this was deeper by an octave and louder, much louder, as it rang, the lights on the boat flickered, the monitors cut out.

Anderton looked worried, "Was that from outside?" A mesmerised Gregory only chuckled and nodded his head. The monitors flickered back into life.

"I've got something, something is moving!" shouted the operator, but the doctor was deadpan,

"OK bring BOB in closer."

"No, you don't understand, look it's moving all around BOB."

Anderton looked at the sonar and it was true, a long dark smudge had appeared all around the position of the submersible. He was no sonar expert but he reckoned the thing was monstrously big. Maybe he would get his story after all. He looked at the monitor showing BOB's camera, the view of the bottom span around, something big was moving the sub.

Anderton looked outside, the loch was flat, perfectly flat. Then, from nowhere, around the boat, there was a large swell.

BANG. The bottom of the boat thumped onto one of the waves. Anderton was starting to become worried.

The doctor noticed,

"Don't worry Mr. Anderton, this is unusual but quite natural, you see the Loch has its very own underwater weather conditions, we are having a storm, that's all."

And sure enough, as Anderton watched, the Loch started to settle as did the camera on the submersible.

"That's one reason everyone thinks that Nessie is here," she said, "there are layers of water at different temperatures, thermoclines, for some reason these slide over each other and cause severe water turbulence. You can see why the locals have, for hundreds of years, thought that something must be in the Loch."

"I've got something else." Said the operator, still excited. "What the hell is that thing, it's too big to be anything that we would normally see but too small for Nessie. Is it a rock? It looks shiny. I reckon it must be twice the size of a man in length. My God, is it walking!"

Anderton's patience was running out,

"What the hell is that thing Gregory?"

"You will find out soon enough, but be careful you'll still have more questions than answers."

The Hindenburg

Germany, March 1937, Tuesday 06:00

Like a predatory shark, it floated there; grey, huge, beautiful, perfect. Almost a living creature which simultaneously generated a cacophony of emotions in the viewer's mind; as a demonstration of man's supremacy over nature it was unrivalled, as an engineering marvel it was supreme, as a symbol Nazi imperialism it was iconic, as a huge bag of explosive gas it was ludicrous. It was the brainchild of a German from an altogether different age; it was a Zeppelin – The Hindenburg. Towards this great ship scurried a ragtag group of passengers and crew, unique in their extremity, these were the apexes of a polarised society.

Captain Eckner and his officers, men of the old empire whose devotion to the Kaiser sat ill with their required adoration of their new leader: a jumped up, syphilis-ridden, Austrian corporal – the dictator Adolf Hitler.

Captain Eckner, the right-hand man of the now dead Count Zeppelin paused momentarily as he peered at the swastika emblazoned on the side of his beloved airship; there was a tangible look of surprise as if he had never seen it before. He looked round quickly to ensure that no one had seen his momentary weakness, but he was greeted by the beaming smile of the leader a group of soldiers. A group with a distasteful love of patent leather, red or black; they were tall and beautiful, muscular and blonde, but an air of fanaticism clung to them like flies on a corpse. They appeared, though in uniform, less like soldiers, more like priests; religious relics and symbolism adorned their bodies like alters: swastikas and skulls, their daggers were more suited to sacrifice than combat. If they were warriors, then they were holy warriors; Knights Templar, spreading the evil religion of Nazism across the world. Their leader, Mörder, beamed enthusiastically at Eckner, not masking his hatred and enjoying

Eckner's obvious discomfort. Eckner quickly nodded and then barked an order to one of his subordinates who rushed off hurriedly. Eckner stood by the boarding stairs greeting his passengers, his Nazi guests got the slightest of a salute, they ignored him as they boarded.

Next came the industrialists and entrepreneurs, grown fat on the manufacturing of arms and the persecution of the Jews; suckling on the teat of Nazism. One day, in the not too distant future, these capitalists would no doubt claim, "it was only business" and accept no responsibility for the genocide they promoted. At the centre of the group was a large fat man in an outlandish fur coat; an American, his name was Blenkinsopp. As he boarded he could be heard loudly deprecating the British government for its faint-heartedness, he abused the States' government for its Isolationism but eulogised on all things German, all things Nazi.

A young man walked quickly to the boarding ladders. He was alone and was looking over his shoulder as if chased by some invisible stalker. He was the son of Eckner and like his father he was an adventurer, but his brand of adventure was mountaineering. Surprisingly he was still dressed in his climbing clothes and was clinging to his large rucksack, which he held guardedly with both hands; his knuckles were white.

"Father!" he shouted and moved towards the ship's captain.

Captain Eckner, face quickly moved from shock to happiness, to that of parental concern.

"Ralf, I thought you were in Greece!"

The two came together; they awkwardly offered hands to shake, then thought better of it and hugged each other.

"I was afraid I'd miss the ship, father."

"Well you cut it close, you were not on the passenger roster twenty minutes ago and to my knowledge the ship is full?" He eyed his son, who habitually got himself into more trouble than the young boy either realised or could cope with.

"Oh, I gave Colonel Mörder a call; he said that he would fix it."

"Did he now?"

Ralf was totally unaware of the passion in his father's voice. He did not understand how a man like his father would feel being told that a Nazi could get Ralf onto the ship that Eckner captained, without Eckner even knowing.

"I've told you before Ralf," Captain Eckner moved his head nearer to his son, "these men are dangerous, keep your distance from them."

Ralf nodded in mock submission, then bounded up the stairs, he was looking forward to a rest on the ship. It had been a busy and dangerous last couple of weeks.

The next to board were a group of about ten Brits, bemoaning bitterly amongst themselves about the German ways, though none would dream of actually complaining. Amongst them were Leslie Charters and his wife, the creator of the super sleuth 'The Saint'; another was a dashing young man just back from Persia and Lord and Lady Rothschild who were chatting amiably to Harold Dick the rep. for 'Goodyear' and 'Zeppelin'.

Last, certainly least and distanced were other businessmen with their families, rich Jews wishing to escape the madness of Europe. For them, it will be a long and unpleasant trip on the Hindenburg, but America would bring security and a chance to live in an unbigoted society – or so they thought.

The last of the fifty passengers climbed the stairs of this behemoth of transport, a ship the size of Titanic, being kept motionless by a handful of tiny figures, clinging to guide ropes. The Hindenburg had just been in for a major re-fit and was making its first scheduled flight of the year to New York, though its departure was surprisingly early in the day. It floated quietly over the tarmac of the landing area for only a few minutes, before the ground crew dropped their ropes and gallons of water dropped from the fuselage. Lighter and un-tethered this monster ship, one moment a beached whale, the next rising magnificently into the air, released from its shackles, it became an agile dolphin.

On board, Captain Eckner, gently pushed through a group of passengers on the promenade, he saw his quarry; Blenkinsopp. He tapped him lightly on the shoulder.

"Mr. Blenkinsopp, perhaps you would like a tour of the ship, I am sure that a man of your engineering background would truly appreciate her."

Blenkinsopp, who on hearing his name, span round grinning and nodded enthusiastically. He was so American, almost 'The American'; a larger than life stereotype in full Technicolor. He had an edge of the south in his accent, he wore a tweed suit and an outrageous Stetson, a large overcoat with thick bear skin collar; the only aspect of his attire missing, to complete the part, was a pair of pistols. He was the American of a comic book, a studied symbol of the west; a dumb patriot, a U.S. of A. cowboy. This studied façade was worn like a mask; the clichéd caricature forced all but the most creative thinkers into a clichéd response; remove his mask and a keen, possibly brilliant mind would be revealed.

"Yeah, Swell." he said.

As predicted, Captain Eckner smiled as you would at a child; Eckner would give Blenkinsopp a tour because the Nazi party was courting the American's support and so he would humour him. Eckner took off at a good pace, describing the ship and pointing out various areas of interest.

"As I am sure you are aware, Mr. Blenkinsopp, the Hindenburg is the biggest ever flying machine built, it is only 23 meters shorter than the Titanic and is itself 244 meters long and at its widest point it has a diameter of 40 meters, with a gas capacity of nearly 1 million cubic meters."

"Gas you say, hydrogen gas?"

Eckner smiled at Blenkinsopp's interruption, he knew where this was going, it may be a floating bomb but the Zeppelins had an unblemished passenger safety record in their long history of service. But the wiley Blenkinsopp was going down another route;

"Why didn't you use Helium?"

Momentarily Eckner's smile fell like his face had been smacked, but his composure quickly reasserted itself.

"Well, whilst Helium is inert, it also has significantly less lift and in fact, the greatest danger on board is the engine fuel, not the hydrogen. We are so confident we have installed a pressurised smoking room on the Hindenburg."

But the real answer was that the USA had developed Helium and owned the world monopoly. The USA refused to let the Zeppelin Company have access, they both knew that – "strike one" for Blenkinsopp. A little more cautiously now Eckner went on:

"Most people think that the gondola hung under the ship is the only useable space, but in fact, we have ample facilities actually within the ships superstructure, on two decks. Both decks are at the bottom of the ship. The upper deck has promenades running down both port and starboard, a dining room, lounge and nearly thirty cabins. On the lower deck, we have toilets, showers, officers' and crew's mess and of course the smoking room."

"Hey, is it true you had a grand piano built for the ship?" Blenkinsopp interjected.

"Not quite a grand Mr. Blenkinsopp, but we do have a special light weight piano for the entertainment of our guests." He waved his hands towards the bow of the ship.

"Forward from the passenger quarters are the mail, radio rooms and officers' quarters; and under these is where the gondola is hung, from which we pilot the ship. Immediately aft of the passenger accommodation is the crew's accommodation, with a second smaller quarters being some 120 meters aft. The ship also has an auxiliary control room aft on the lower fin, just above the landing wheel."

At this point, Eckner had reached the bottom of a flight of stairs which took the pair to the lower or B deck. They walked past doors, signed as toilets and came to a door marked "Smoking room", he opened it but behind it were two further doors at right angles to each other. In front, the door said, "Crew Only."

"As you can see, Mr. Blenkinsopp, here is our smoking room, but I have something much better to show you." With that, he opened the "Crew only" door and stepped through into a seemingly uninteresting wide corridor. As Blenkinsopp stepped through he realised that he was in the keel corridor, the main artery of the ship; looking forward he could see the equivalent of the width of a football pitch, after which the corridor, following the natural curve of the bow was hidden. Looking aft the corridor ran for what looked like infinity, though he calculated it must be two football pitches long. For a moment he was truly struck by the awesome human achievement that the ship represented and could only say;

"Please show me more."

Eckner, satisfied with the obvious awe that was evident on Blenkinsopp's face, led him aft about 15 steps. There were the huge fuel, oil and water tanks, but he had saved the best for last, he pointed up. Blenkinsopp's followed the gaze of Eckner and saw the vertical access-shaft, the height of a man in diameter, with a ladder running up it for some 35 meters and at the top daylight.

"Our crew have gone up these and repaired the skin of the ship whilst airborne!"

"You are kidding, right?"

"No, Mr. Blenkinsopp I am not kidding", said the smiling Eckner, "there is a guide rope that leads from stern to aft, from here you have access to the other shafts. My men have been up there in all weathers, it is a fine crew that we have on this ship."

Blenkinsopp, now back it character, simply said

"I don't doubt it Sir, let me buy you a drink."

The Competition

Marine Training Centre with Major Lance.

"Are you ready?" Barks a young drill sergeant.

"Yeah." I reply and step onto the mats.

It does not matter whether you are a club wielding cave man or a high-tech soldier, sooner or later it comes down to this – one on one, flesh and bone, tooth and nail. I've killed so many, in so many different ways and probably achieved bugger all, except for a few broken hearts. Once a year, I come here, the Marine grappling competition. It's a test, can I still do it? Am I fit enough, strong enough, tough enough? We will see.

I am kneeling, facing my opponent – God they get younger every year – I swear one day they will be wearing nappies. My opponent is one of those lean wiry types, you can tell he is strong, but endurance will be his game. Me, I'm a survivor, I like to keep some spare fat around my waist – you know – just in case! Anyway, it will lull this young fool it to thinking that I am easy meat.

A sergeant bellows "Go" and we are off. We both shuffle forward, eyeing each other intensely; slowly we reach out to grab each other's shoulders. Bang. What the Hell? While I am busy day dreaming, he moves like lightning, smacks his biceps into the side of my neck and takes me down into a headlock. A great start! A strike like that really scrambles your eggs – I've got to respond and quickly. But not quick enough, he has moved into the "mount"; this is just like the schoolyard fights, he is kneeling over my chest, he has one arm behind my head, the other across my throat, each of his hands grips the elbow of the other arm and with this vice like grip he starts to squeeze. I turn my head, it should help to reduce the pressure on my throat, it doesn't! When you are in a lock like this, it is almost spiritual, you are scared, your breathing starts to become ragged and slowly, ever so slowly things go out of focus, then the colour seems to drain from your vision, particularly around the edges, then you really lose the plot as a mad painter splashes blackness everywhere. It is spiritual; I wonder if this is what it is like to die?

"Aarrgh", the scream rouses me from my reverie; better yet it's not me screaming. Is it training, is it arrogance, is it a sixth sense? Whatever, whilst quietly blacking out I slipped my hand down and illegally grabbed a hand full of his bollocks. He loses his concentration and his grip relaxes. The door has opened, only a crack, but it's a crack I intend to make use of it by jamming in my knee. I pin his arms, arch my back and look over my shoulder and off he flies, it is my turn to be quick. I roll onto to him into the mount, he pushes up trying to reach my throat, bad mistake. I whip my backside around to my left, wrap my left leg around his arm which is still in the air and then lean back. I have his arm bending backwards between my legs, which are both across his chest, it is all over and he taps out.

22 years in the marines, I am definitely getting too old for this shit.

Ten fights later and I exit the competition. I get fourth, not bad for a man fighting guys half my age. Besides this sort of fight is only a rehearsal. Here, there are rules and boundaries that cannot be broken. Some are written, like 'You cannot punch', obviously everybody does, but only sneaky little digs. The more important rules are the ones in your head; they are the boundaries that rational people don't cross. Would you break some one's nose to win a competition, or how about an arm, or a leg, or a back, or perhaps just kill them dead? The Masters said that you must embrace death and be equally ready to lose your own life as to take another and in part, I believe that. Wars for the main are fought by normal people, who value their life because they've got one, they have a family, friends. War is a temporary imposition on them, one that they are desperate to return from. These types don't win wars, guys like me win wars. We don't value life, not other peoples, not our own. War to me is an adrenaline rush, to put it bluntly, you have to break eggs to make an omelette, do you then feel sorry for the eggs? No and neither do I. I don't believe in heroes, heroes are killers, they are not brave because they have nothing to lose.

So, as I said, these competitions are just rehearsals, they test your speed, your fitness and your technique, but outside, out there in the real world, I would kill any of competitors in seconds.

By now I am back in the changing rooms, getting changed and like all men, I can't help but flex a few muscles in the mirror. I am in good shape, I run 10 miles a day and do God knows how many sports. I smile wickedly at myself – I do alright with the girls if they like the rough type: green eyes, crooked nose, square jaw, my hair is egg shell blond, so I wear what I have left short, very short. I look closely at the mirror, my body is like a road map to the last 20 years of international politics, I've got a scar for nearly every war I've been in, officially or unofficially. The worst is from the last job, the angry red jagged lines of a shrapnel scar run raggedly from my chest and over my clavicle. I wince as I remember the pain.

In the battalion I am a full-blooded war veteran hero, Death and Glory, I have had both. But as I look at myself in the mirror, my grin drops away from my face like a distant memory. What do I think about it all, honestly? I am totally pissed off. All my greatest achievements have been death and destruction, even when I have saved lives it has cost somebody else theirs. It's time for a career change – I am going take up gardening.

The Flight

After an excellent lunch, the passengers were taking in the view on the promenade on a crisp spring afternoon. Blenkinsopp moved over to join a young English gentleman, who was absentmindedly gazing at several geese flying in formation.

"Beautiful aren't they?" The Englishman said without looking at Blenkinsopp.

"Yeah, that they are."

The pair stood there admiring the birds for some moments.

"Did you see any eagles whilst in Germany; they say it is one of the best places on earth to see them?" It was a simple question from Blenkinsopp.

The young man turned casually, but the experienced Blenkinsopp saw how his knuckles whitened around the rail on which he was leaning. Blenkinsopp mused to himself that his friend was still young, but in this game, age was a luxury very few came to enjoy.

"No, I saw many Hawks, but no Eagles", the young man extended his hand, "my name is John Lazenby."

"Abe…..Abe Blenkinsopp Junior." Blenkinsopp shook his hand warmly. To the casual observer the two were newly met, but for them, this is the first genuine contact in months, the first of complete trust, something solid that they could hold onto for the coming difficult weeks.

Blenkinsopp was a veteran in the spying game, overly idealistic but effective. He was a rare character in many ways, a brilliant engineer, a patriot and a man who despite ten years in the spying game was still an optimist and a lover of mankind. Lazenby was as different to Blenkinsopp as 'Black is to White'. He was tall and muscular with dark hair, centre parted with a waterfall of locks cascading down to his almond eyes, with his olive tan he could have passed as Italian. He was one of the Etonian public school British Officers, so merrily slaughtered in the Great War. He had already seen active service, though much of it unofficially, particularly in the Middle East. In Persia, he had served for a while with the Rifle Brigade and it was whilst in Persia that he had first started his career in the hidden wars, flying as a 'civy' to map the geology of the area. The reality was the British were creating accurate maps for the coming war. He and Blenkinsopp were politically and geographically an ocean apart and could not agree on a single view, but they were both deeply patriotic and totally anti-Nazi. They were friends and after their last dangerous mission together, they trusted each other completely.

Blenkinsopp casually looked around ensuring that no one was in earshot, "So what's so important that you needed me to get on this thing, you know I don't like flying!"

Lazenby never took his eyes off the panoramic view, "Do you see the young chap in the tweeds, talking to the Nazi, HE is the reason!"

"Why that is Young Eckner, are you sure, always figured him as being straight, he's no spy. Mind you, I don't like his idea of company, the fellow with him isn't just any Nazi, that is Mörder and he is the real McCoy. What do you have on Young Eckner?"

"A chance encounter really, on my way back from Persia I was passing through Greece and took a week off to do a bit of sightseeing, you know how I like my archaeology. Anyway, I was in a small town in the North called Thessaloniki, do you know it?"

"I am from the States, not Mars, I know where it is!"

"Err... Sorry old boy. Anyway, I was sitting in the hotel bar, only decent one there, when in walks our friend there, climbing kit and all."

"Yeah, so he is a mountaineer and Greece is full of mountains."

Lazenby smiled at Blenkinsopp, he liked his dry humour.

"Yes, but that night news came from Halkidiki that someone had murdered a monk. Now I didn't think anything of it then…."

"Wait a minute, I may know where Thessaloniki is but what the hell is Halkidiki?" said Blenkinsopp, starting to show signs of impatience.

"It's the three fingers of land pointing into the sea, they are all very mountainous, but one, Athos, is the home of Greek orthodox monks. No women are allowed on the entire peninsula. These are some of the oldest monasteries in the world, holding an untold amount of artefacts and most of them are on the tops of mountains."

"Right…… I see where you are going with this, but you didn't get me on this bag of gas to tell me about a guy who climbs mountains to murder monks – what else is there?"

Lazenby took a breath ready to deliver his news, the news that he had carried alone for two weeks.

"It's the Greater Key of Solomon!"

But if he expected to get any reaction from Blenkinsopp, he didn't get one, particularly with this mumbo jumbo. Blenkinsopp shook his head,

"I preferred your 'monk murdering mountaineer' story, go on tell me what in God's name is the Greater Key of Solomon."

But Lazenby was nodding his head,

"That's the point, it's not in God's name, it's in Satan's. The monks were said to have kept a terrible book, which contains the summonations to bring demons and devils into this world. That's what the Key of Solomon is, it's a book of Black magic, may be THE book of Black magic and someone climbed a four hundred foot cliff, broke into a monastery and murdered a monk to get it."

Blenkinsopp for the first time showed real interest.

"Yeah, there are not many who could make that sort of climb. Now we know Hitler is into the Arcane, but surely not even he is cracked pot enough to think that it will actually work."

Lazenby, worry etched on his face, said.

"He IS that much of a crackpot! And if he gets an edge, even one that he is imagining, then it might be enough to push him into war."

Blenkinsopp pulled a face like he was chewing a wasp. His religion was science and the thought that someone existed who might plunge the world into a war because he thought he could control demons, scared him silly.

"So why are we going to America", it was a rhetorical question and one his keen mind quickly answers, "Crowley, he is going to see Aleister Crowley for a translation. Hum, well, not while I live he ain't. Well done Lazenby, that's a good bit of work." Blenkinsopp turned to go but then clearly thought of something else.

"I'd put this down to idle gossip, but when I said Mörder wasn't just any old Nazi, I meant it. Rumour has it that he is the head of a Nazi Masonic lodge but for kicks, these guys don't do dodgy handshakes, these guys do virgins and worse. They say that Hitler himself comes to the ceremonies, I should think that if Young Eckner and Mörder are together, then that just about confirms your story."

Blenkinsopp turned and headed for the bar, partly in character, but this time for once he actually needed a strong drink.

The Hindenburg had been making steady progress through the day. The route was to be from Berlin, a northwesterly path, up the coast of Denmark, across the straits to Norway, then turning east at Stavanger, Faroes, Iceland, then to Greenland. Once land was picked up, she would follow the east coast of Canada down to the States and eventually New York. This route benefited the Hindenburg as she could make maximum use of the favourable winds and progress should be good, averaging 80 mph; a blistering pace when compared to an ocean liner. In the morning at around 12:00 the ship had moved off land into the North Sea and the passengers were looking forward to the sight of the Faroes.

"Fancy a smoke old boy", asked Lazenby, already turning to the stairs and heading for the smoking room. Blenkinsopp nodded and they were both about to descend the stairs onto B Deck; when their attention was taken by a rather curt cough. They both turned to face, two officers of the SS, accompanied by Young Eckner. Despite himself Lazenby's mind raced, but his friend seemed totally at ease.

"Hey Mörder, how you doing buddy?"

"Very well indeed Mr. Blenkinsopp, may I introduce my… how do you say 'Right-hand man', this is Kruger and this is the world famous mountaineer Mr. Eckner."

Kruger, though a less impressive model of Arian soldiery, was another German blonde, decked in black leather and stinking of Nazism; but while Mörder carried his outfit nobly, like the black night, Kruger stooped and looked perverse. Kruger snapped his heels and lifted his arm in Nazi salute.

"Heil Hitler."

"Yeah, Heil." Blenkinsopp barely lifted his wrist in response.

"I believe Mr. Blenkinsopp," the words dripped from Kruger's mouth, "that you have been to my hometown, München."

"Yeah, Bavaria is a lovely part of the world."

"And who is our friend?" Though Kruger tried to be polite, it sounded like an interrogation.

"I'm sorry, where are my manners, this fellow is John Lazenby, I just met him today, he is on his way back from Persia." Then facing Lazenby, "Can I introduce you to Major Enrich and Captain Kruger of the SS and this young man is Mr. Eckner – 'Junior' I believe."

As Kruger cocked his arm for another Heil Hitler, Lazenby beat him to the drop, with a hand thrust out for a more civilised handshake.

"Pleased to meet you old boy."

Kruger dropped his arm, but instead of shaking Lazenby's hand, just nodded irritably.

"Ah, English."

Lazenby refused to lower his hand and the impasse was only broken when Young Eckner stepped in and grasped Lazenby's hand and shook it saying:

"I hope you are enjoying your flight on the world's greatest aircraft, did Mr. Blenkinsopp say you have just come back from Persia, I myself have just returned from Greece."

Lazenby was not comfortable talking to what he considered being the enemy; he had not yet developed Blenkinsopp's easy manners.

"Yes, I was out there surveying for oil and yourself what were you doing in Greece?"

An infectious smile spread across Young Eckner's face, "Oh, exactly the same as you and I didn't find any oil either."

Though both men were on the surface cordial their eyes bored into one another, each testing the other. But Lazenby's mind was racing, what had Young Eckner meant, should he be taken on face value, did he know about mapping, or was he talking about spying?

Blenkinsopp piped in, "We are off for a smoke, would you gentlemen like to join us?"

"No thank you, Mr. Blenkinsopp, but please you continue." replied Mörder

With that, Lazenby and Blenkinsopp descended the stairs, leaving the three Germans alone.

Mörder looked at Kruger. "You are too easily upset Kruger, don't show your anger so easily. I do not like this Mr. Lazenby, I want you to watch him. Closely. Now Eckner you have the package?"

"Yes"

"Then bring it to the port store room at 03:00 hrs. Tonight I will attempt the first incantation."

Meanwhile, Lazenby and Blenkinsopp had continued to the smoking room. They had passed the ablutions, through a door, then knocked on the next door and waited for the steward to let them in. Lazenby offered Blenkinsopp a Woodbine; Blenkinsopp looked pained at such a poor smoke. He reached inside his coat pocket and produces a huge cigar container.

"Cuban, my friend?"

Lazenby smiled and accepted the cigar and asked,

"I don't like those two Nazis, even less than Eckner, do you think that they are watching us?"

"Us, no. You, yes; and you would do well not to annoy Kruger, he has a reputation."

But before he could expand on this; the door in front of them opened with a notable hiss. The head steward welcomed them the pair in, through the bar and into the smoking room, where already a dense layer of smoke had formed above the eight or nine passengers. Blenkinsopp, a veteran of the Hindenburg after his tour, explained how the room was pressurised to ensure no hydrogen could get in and passed Lazenby the Hindenburg lighter, the only one allowed on board.

After an hour in the smoking room, Blenkinsopp and Lazenby left and avoided each other for most of the afternoon, not wishing to be seen as anything more than casual acquaintances. But about an hour and a half before dusk, they reconvened with several other passengers on the promenade. They were hoping to catch a glimpse of the some of the Islands around northern Scotland through the clouds.

Alongside them were Lord and Lady Rothschild, staunchly patriotic to King and country, though having both been born and raised in the jewel in the crown – India, with no more than a handful of months spent in good old Blighty. With the group were two American reporters from New York, homeward bound after doing six months in Berlin. Blenkinsopp, always in role, started arguing forcibly about the benefits of Nazism and the failing of the USA to enter world politics; this done mainly for the benefit of Enrich, who was swaggering, just out of earshot.

One of the reporters, who went by the solid American name of Luchelsky, looked very uncomfortable. He had a slight stoop, his fingers danced nervously in the space that his confiscated camera would normally hang at all times; other than when he was sleeping. He had been quite animated that morning when boarding the ship, to be told that flashlights and airships didn't mix well, he was like a cripple without crutches. Blenkinsopp played him like a piano, moving progressively up the scales; Luchelsky could take no more.

"Call yourself an American, why if we weren't in the presence of a lady, I'd punch you right in the eye."

Lady Rothschild who could imagine few spectacles of more satisfaction, than seeing a member of the press punching a Nazi sympathiser and both Americans, to boot, grinned and said,

"Please Gentlemen, I have four brothers, don't let me stop you."

Blenkinsopp smiled wryly at her, flashing a nicotine stained smile, then squared with the reporter. He was sure he could push this fellow a little further yet; he had found from experience that those who are going to hit you - hit you; they never talked about it.

Luchelsky looked back dumbly, his options having rapidly narrowed. The impasse was broken suddenly when over the ships intercom came an announcement; first in German and then in English.

"Ladies and Gentlemen, we may experience some turbulence for the next hour, we hope that this does not cause you any inconvenience, thank you."

Lazenby looked out of the windows and then back at his company with a confused look on his face:

"Odd, I can't see any reason for turbulence" as he scanned the clear sky, "unless we are going to drop into the cloud below."

He then turned to face his group and noticed a momentary frown from Blenkinsopp. Lazenby thought he too must be confused by the announcement, but then realised his error; he was new to this game and Blenkinsopp was still helping to refine his skills. The art of the spy was to be the grey talentless man, who never spots the exceptional.

"Aah, what do you know about the weather, first time off the floor ain't it" Blenkinsopp lied fluently and then to further calm nerves he turned to Luchelsky;

"Hell, let's go get a good shot of American bourbon."

About 15 minutes later the passengers were in a lively debate about the German Olympics, whilst the two spies looked out over the clouds. Blenkinsopp said in soft muffled tones,

"Lazenby, your ears are better than mine, can you hear that?"

For the last few minutes, above the tones of the lightweight aluminium Zeppelin piano and the constant drone of the ship's engines could be heard a higher pitched tone. Then from nowhere, the ship jumped higher in the air.

"Ooh", a surprised Lady Rothschild shouted, then beamed at Lazenby,

"Well, there is your turbulence, Mr. Lazenby."

Then with the roar of an engine, a biplane appeared, just below off the Port bow.

"By Jove, it's the RAF, it's a Gladiator", beamed an ecstatic Lord Rothschild and then to Mörder,

"Just checking up on you, no doubt."

Enrich, out of character for him, smiled and nodded in agreement.

"I think it's a Gloster Gladiator", Lazenby said for the passenger's benefit, then very quietly for Blenkinsopp,

"If it wasn't a German Henschel, in RAF paint, with a roof on. I would say that that could have come from only one place and is going to only one place."

Blenkinsopp turned to him gravely, "Are you thinking of the Macon?"

"Yes, the Macon."

The Walk

Off the Greenland Coast on the Hindenburg, March 1937, Wednesday 03:00 hrs.

The Germans were not the only super power to use airships, all the major powers had at least tinkered. The Americans were particularly interested in the airship, as it had thousands of miles of coast which needed to be patrolled. A visionary concept, lead finally to the design of the Macon, a huge airship with a maximum speed of 87 miles per hour. But what was really amazing about her, was that she was an aircraft carrier. Sitting inside her underbelly were five Sparrow Hawk fighter aircraft, which could be launched and then landed by use of a long hook. The Macon had crashed in '34 and as new generations of fighters hit production the requirement diminished; these new aircraft had a much greater range and rendered the whole carrier idea obsolete.

If the Germans could launch an aircraft from the Hindenburg, it could be put to all sorts of clandestine work. As Lord Rothschild had quickly decided that the plane was RAF, so too would even the most experienced of viewers; for where else could a plane with a 300 miles range come from, it must be British. This would leave all British military, radar and naval installations, wide open to close reconnaissance and aerial photography. When the aircraft had been dropped, they were in range of Orkney Islands. These islands, just off the North East coast of Scotland, formed a natural deep water harbour and it was where the Royal Navy anchored the Grand Fleet. The Royal Navy were particularly worried about U-boat submarines navigating through the sand banks and submarine nets into the harbour and wreaking havoc It was, therefore, vital that Lazenby destroyed any photos that the aircraft had taken.

Earlier in the evening after the plane had first been seen, the noise of the engine reappeared, though most of the passengers were dining and were blissfully unaware. Even when the slight jolt occurred, with what Lazenby assumed must have been the re-coupling, the passengers munched on merrily. The second jolt was closely followed by another broadcast by the Captain informing everybody that the turbulence had passed. Lazenby had wondered how often they could get away with that ruse.

After dinner, there was inevitably a lot of drinking and it was not until nearly one in the morning that the last passengers emptied their glasses and retired. The Hindenburg was nearing the coast of Greenland and would soon turn south towards the States.

Lazenby had waited till three before venturing from his room. He slowly opened the door from his berth and stepped into the corridor. The passenger's quarters were laid out in four rows, all with access to either one of the promenades or the central corridor. Lazenby carefully looked up and down the corridor. There was a solitary light showing from a room at the other end of the corridor, but other than that nothing stirred. Lazenby had no idea whose room it was, most likely it would be someone on a late night triste. The Hindenburg was in many ways like a sea-going ship, there was that constant noise and vibration caused by the engines. All the passengers had soon become unaware of this background drone, but never the less it was there, so even the relatively thin walls of the berths offered a good level of privacy. The noise also masked the movements of Lazenby, whilst he sneaked towards the bow of the ship and access to B Deck.

Lazenby needed to get to the central corridor of the ship to be able to move aft, where the aircraft was almost certainly hangered. He was safe whilst in the passenger section, but once he was in the corridor he would be playing for quite different stakes. He moved silently down the stairs, past the toilets, with the quickest of glances out of the port windows; but the view was so stunning he paused a while.

It was a crystal clear night and the billion stars in the bright Milky Way twinkled and reflected in the vast, dark, deep Atlantic Ocean below. In the darkness, without the usual light pollution of city life; the night sky was almost bright. Below the great Atlantic Ocean was still, its mirror-like dark surface reflecting the celestial light. Despite himself, a shudder passed involuntarily down his body. Odd he thought, creeping around under a bag of explosive hydrogen, fighting a clandestine war with Nazism had little effect on his mood; looking into the depths of space and the more immediate ocean below, unnerved him deeply. He momentarily imagined what it would be like to be bobbing alone in that ocean, the vastness of the Atlantic confounded his keen mind. He made a mental note never to go sailing and moved on.

He came to the end of the corridor and paused at the door. He needed to be quiet as the chief steward was sleeping, just behind the thin wall. He opened the door marked 'Forbidden', with a quick check fore and aft and stepped into the dark and chilly corridor.

Lazenby was not important enough for a Nazi guided tour so this was his first opportunity to see the ship – it was stunning! The corridor ran fore and aft in the ship literally as far as the eye could see. Forward it curved up with the ship hull, aft it ran for what looked like miles, lit every ten paces by small night lights. A sudden lightning strike of fear ripped through his body, how on earth could he get down that without being seen?

Despite the night lights, it was dimmer here than in the main ship and he waited for his eyes to adjust. Just as he had been taught at infantry sky, he cupped his ear with his hand and opened his mouth to improve his hearing. To improve his sight he looked away and used his peripheral vision and soon, he started to see other shapes. The corridor was not simply enclosed like the passenger sections; it was edged by great aluminium girders. Above, were the bottom of the huge hydrogen bags that held the ship in the air. The main corridor was a series of girders forming a large triangle, hundreds of them. Only a few steps ahead, the wooden internal wall ended, beyond that he could see large open spaces inside the ship's hull. Stacked in these spaces were a variety of storage boxes and arranged more formally huge tanks, he assumed for water, fuel, oil and hydrogen.

He moved aft to the edge of the passenger quarters and realised that he was on a metallic walkway. He knelt down, reached out and was shocked that he could touch the cloth of the outer hull of the ship. What was more alarming, were the gaps between the sections; which were bound together with rope, with a good arm's length between each. The whole affair reminded him of tip toeing in a loft, the crisscrossing metal supports and gangways were like the joists, but should you miss a step here you would put your foot through the floor – an extremely bad idea in an airship.

As his hand was still resting on the metal grid of the gangway below him, he felt rather than heard, the footsteps coming from behind him. His immediate thought was that he had been seen and he wheeled around ready to fight, but as he did so he could only see the feet of a man in the distance. As the corridor curved upward towards the bow, the rest of the man was obscured by the ceiling. Quick as a cat, Lazenby leapt behind one of the large tanks, easily as tall as him. As the man neared, Lazenby realised by the sound of the footsteps, that there were, in fact, two men. They were changing watch in the control gondola forward. He had been lucky; these two men must have been relieved by two others if he had tried to move up the corridor five minutes earlier he would probably have walked straight into them. He watched the men move about 50 steps aft, they then exited the corridor on the port side into the crew quarters.

Lazenby waited for a minute, then started to move briskly down the corridor. Intermittently he passed a vertical shaft which went right through the ship up and down. He passed the crew quarters and moved onto the stern. He was pretty sure that they would be no crew this far back on the ship, at this time of night; though he did not relax. His mind was constantly analysing his surroundings, where could he hide, where could he escape to, what if he were cut off, all with professional efficiency. He came to another vertical shaft to his right. Further down the corridor, on both sides, there were large double doors. One of these rooms would hold the aircraft, but then he noticed a single door in the recess of the shaft. He silently moved to the door and put his ear to it; he heard no noise. He was starting to reach for the handle when he suddenly stopped; something was wrong. Lazenby was vaguely religious and had been brought up a Christian, but whilst he believed, he was never really sure, he had little Faith. In truth, he knew more about Hellenic Gods than his own. He viewed the modern evils of witches, the Green man the cloven hoof Satan with the same academic interest of that of the Greek evils of Medusa, Minotaur and Charon. But standing, hand poised to open the door, he felt something malevolent. Inexplicitly, as real as a breeze on his face, he felt a gust of pure evil wash over his back. His heart started pumping as if he was running for his life, sweat ran down his back, hairs stood on end. He stood there like a drowning man and like a drowning man he reached for the ladder and climbed. After eight rungs of the ladder he hugged the ladder and gasped for air, then he heard the footsteps coming down the corridor.

There was a slight gap behind the ladder into which he squeezed half his body and this shielded him from direct gaze from below, though he could still crane his head and see along the corridor. As he clung there, he concentrated on his breathing, which even with the background thrum of the engines, sounded to his ears like large bellows. He took deep breaths, quietly and tried to calm down.

When he first saw the person, he was probably no more than 15 steps away and the man was walking towards him; he could clearly hear each footfall on the steel floor. With each step his tension rose, it was as if death himself was approaching. Then he started to panic, "What if he looks up, will he be able to see me, no I am safe here, don't be mad he will easily see me"; round and round his mind argued with itself. With each step, Lazenby became more fixated that the man would stop and look up and then all would be lost. Still, the man's footsteps rang out below, he was close now, surely any second, but the man took at least another ten steps and sounder no closer and still the footsteps rang out.

Then he was there and the man did stop. Lazenby stopped breathing, he could hear his own heartbeat, banging in his ears, like a policeman banging on a door. His head stuck out from the ladder, in full view if the man looked up he would be caught; but he could no sooner move his head back than he could fly. But the man standing below him was none other than Young Eckner, he did not look up, Eckner's mind was in a darker place. Under his arm he held a large bundle wrapped in a velvet cloth; and surely inside was the Greater Key of Solomon, the most evil book in the known world. Lazenby could have moved his foot and touched Eckner on the head, so close were the men. It was a surreal moment for Lazenby, he was a voyeur to a private moment of Eckner's life, a weak moment, a moment full of fear. Just as Lazenby had been, only a moment earlier, there was Eckner, panting although he had been walking slowly, beads of perspiration on his forehead. Lazenby witnessed a man who had conquered mountains, a man who had calmly scaled a massive vertical rock face and slew an innocent monk and yet was standing in a blind panic. Eckner was a match for it though, he raised himself up and moved on up the corridor.

"Where've you been!" whispered another voice from just below which ripped through the silence like a tornado, the shock of it nearly unseating Lazenby.

"Quick get inside." Said the voice.

Lazenby heard footsteps and a heavy door slid shut. He realised then how close he had come, a few more steps forward and he would have walked straight into this third man. The door must only have been a few feet past from his shaft. Lazenby, now the master of his fear, decided that whatever was going to happen in this room he should take a moment to check it out.

The Hindenburg was primarily made of its superstructure and gas bags and whilst all the passenger rooms were fully fitted out, most other areas were just surrounded by those bags. With a little effort, Lazenby was able to push and crawl less than half his height and gain a vantage point into the room that the two men had just entered. He quietly hauled some canvass material out of the way and was initially disappointed to see only a storage room. The area was about the size of a tennis court, filled with various boxes and other packaging. In the centre was a large crane device, or davit, like those used for life rafts, connected to a winch above a large pair of trap doors. From the davit hung a finger thick metal hawser, with a large hook on the end, for lifting stores into the room.

Standing in a cleared area in front of the crane was the very unhappy Young Eckner and Mörder, who was still immaculately dressed in full SS regalia. They were in the middle of a heated debate, which Lazenby had missed whilst he was getting into position.

"What do you mean?" asked an angry Mörder.

"I didn't want any of this"

"You got the book didn't you, what did you think we would do with it?"

"I got the book because I was following orders, I was told it would have a psychological effect on the Jews!"

Mörder face fell into an ugly smile,

"Oh, it will have more than psychological effect!" His smile was twice as threatening because it was so false.

"Take your book I am having nothing to do with this shit!"

With that Eckner threw the book at Mörder, span round and was gone. Mörder dived for the book; as if it was a dropped newborn baby. All thought of Eckner was immediately gone, as he fawned and pawed the book, stroking it almost sexually. He spun around and looked for somewhere to rest it and recklessly swept the top of a large packing box with his arm, the various items dropping with a clang onto the floor. He then laid the book down onto the box, like a new bride onto a bed and with equal enthusiasm stripped his bride of the velvet cloth.

Under the cloth was an ancient book, that much Lazenby could see; leather bound, heavy metal clasp and with much gold inlay. But as Lazenby laid his eyes on that book it was as if the evil in it reached out and smacked him in the face, it was that tangible. Lazenby smelled the evil, he could taste the evil and though a rational man, he wanted to run and hide. But another side of him, a darker side, wanted to join with the book. He watched Mörder tenderly caressing the book and for a moment he wanted to kill Mörder, for who did Mörder think he was, touching his book. The thought lasted only a moment and was gone, but its stain would stay with Lazenby throughout his natural life.

Mörder seemed temporarily satiated and stood up, he reached down behind a packing crate and stood back up with a large white sheet which he pulled over his head. It was only then that Lazenby saw what it was, Mörder had donned the outfit better suited to the Spanish Inquisition and in modern times the 'Ku Klux Klan'. He stood there resplendent in a white silk suit with a large pointed mask covering all his face bar for two small eye holes. Next, he produced a large white cockerel and a ludicrously impractical knife and like a scene from some nightmare slit the chicken's throat. With its blood dripping down his arm and soiling his immaculate white outfit, he drew out a pentagon surrounded by a circle. Accompanying all of this was a strange guttural chant, it was a language not like anything Lazenby knew. He had had a public school education and was good with languages, Latin, Greek, French, German even some Italian and Spanish and a little Persian, but he had never heard a language like this one. Lazenby watched aghast; as this ghoulish theatre was acted out before him.

Mörder, went to the centre of the pentagon and with the book in hand started a complex ceremony. A summonation to bring the vile evil from hell; Mörder was calling forth the swarm of Satan spawn.

But this was not the time or place for Lazenby to act, as he left he uttered under his breath,

"As God is my witness, that book will burn!"

He returned to the ladder and lowered himself down. He was pretty sure that the aircraft must be in the cargo bay across the corridor. He walked to the door clearly marked in German as 'Storage'. The port one he could still hear Mörder chanting but Lazenby's quarry was the aircraft.

He slid the door open and sure enough there she was – the Henschel HS123. She was good looking, a classic biplane with a huge, powerful looking BMW power plant. Underneath she had fixed carriages, but their forward angle and swept back covers gave them the appearance of talons and the whole plane that of an eagle. In '35 she was the Luftwaffe's newest recruit, but she was already becoming obsolete with the new generation of single wing aircraft, like the Messerschmitt BF 109 being delivered in their droves. It was odd looking at the plane, with added canopy and RAF decals to mimic that of the Gloster Gladiator, an aircraft he had flown and known intimately. The plane was hung from a davit and was lashed to the deck to stop her moving. This davit was a more complex affair than the norm, with several arms allowing it to be extended forward and out of the ship. Directly in front of the plane was a large area covered by a concertinaed hatch, which looked extremely flimsy. The hatch could be folded up, the davit extended forward through the hole, the plane could then match the speed of airship and be unhooked. Thinking of it gave Lazenby a momentary thrill; as he imagined what that must be like. Landing would be the reverse of the process.

Lazenby turned his attention to the plane. It would be pointless to disable it. Once he reported it, the whole idea would be defunct, the RAF would simply escort the airship whenever near home waters. He cast his knowledgeable eyes over the plane, he was somehow disturbed to see it was armed with guns, but he soon found what he was looking for. On the plane was a camera, mounted on a bomb rack, it was crude but did its job. Lazenby went to check if there was still any film in it; aerial photography of Scapa Flow would furnish a U-Boat with just the information to get into the sound and do some very serious damage. Scapa Flow was Britain's safest natural harbour, not unlike Pearl Harbour, but much colder.

The camera was operated by a wire trigger which wound into the cockpit, just like one used on any normal camera but longer. Lazenby unscrewed it and then un-sprung the supports holding the camera to the bomb rack. But it took some time, it was several minutes before he carried the camera over to a bench and started to unscrew the base.

"Well, Mr. Lazenby what would...."

SLAM

On hearing the words from somebody only an arm's reach behind him, Lazenby, with cat-like reflex, whirled the camera around like a bat and smashed the man in the face. The blow caught the man full force and knocked him against a stanchion. Lazenby never hesitated, he immediately struck again.

CRUNCH

This time the head, resting against the metal support had nowhere to go and cracked open with a sickening noise, like a melon being dropped from a height. Lazenby had learnt from bitter experience that people in his line of work needed to take the initiative. He looked at the body, it was wearing the black uniform of the SS and was still clutching a Lugar pistol. It could be only one man – Mörder, he was of the right build, but the bloodied mess that was his head was impossible to identify. Lazenby could imagine how Mörder would deliver his clever line, like a 'super spy' or 'spy catcher'; but this was the real world.

Lazenby quickly opened the hatch. He had hoped to simply remove the film and leave no trace, that was no longer possible, but he could maybe cover his tracks. He threw the camera out of the hatch. He found a tarpaulin, tentatively wrapped it around Mörder so as not to get any blood or mush on him and dragged him feet first to the hatch, then kicked him out. He found a blanket, mopped up the mess, smeared a little grease over the area and threw the blanket out, it was a reasonable cover up. Still lying on the floor was the Lugar, he picked it up ready to throw it out, then paused; it would be a good idea to hide all evidence of Mörder – he might have fallen overboard or even jumped. This gun would be a link if found on Lazenby. Foul play would be immediately suspected; but a gun might be very useful. Emotion conquered logic and he slid the gun into his trouser pocket. A minute later he had closed all the hatches and was on his way back up the corridor. Just before he reached the passengers' quarters he slid the Lugar under a support bracket of the last water tank and made his way back to his room.

Tomorrow he thought there would be some questions, but what could the Germans do. To charge someone they would have to admit to the aircraft, with the next stop being New York, it would be American Police searching the plane. As long as they kept going west he was safe, as long as the Hindenburg continued to head west, he was safe.

The Pole

In this landscape there are only two tones, the white of the ice and the black of the night sky, it is the North Pole. Mile upon mile of broken ice packs, stack one upon the next, this is an impassable terrain, this is an unforgiving terrain, this place is death! In the fey light stretches this fairie kingdom of towering minuets, colossal castles and epic cathedrals. It is the domain of the Norse Alfar and Trolls, here it is that the mighty Aesir and Vanir will fight the giants in the last desperate battle to save the world and in the battle of all battles, Ragnarok, the world will end. The minuets however are made only of ice, the castles and cathedrals too, are simply monumental slabs and the battle of Ragnarok is only folklore. But the evil which now comes to the Pole is real and is not folklore.

A small red burning globe appears in the sky, burning as if Satan himself has come into the world, summoned by incantation on the not so distant Hindenburg. The demonic flame grows in size, as it comes closer. Suddenly there is a great sonic boom and a new colour is added to the palette. Now burning across the sky, in vulgar orange is the tale of a meteorite. At its fore is a seemingly minute pinhead of raw rock, it burns and glows like something spat from Vulcan's workshop.

The meteorite arches to earth where it impacts with a huge plume of ice, which shoots high into the sky. The rock itself is not great, perhaps the size of a small house, but it has created an elliptical shaped impact crater, the size of a football stadium. In the centre the boulder sits, its great heat soon forms a puddle from the ice, then a pond and finally a lake, into which the rock sinks.

Already the rock has lost its red glow, to orange, to brown. In the elemental struggle, the cold of the ice pack defeats the raw heat of the meteorite and quickly the rock is cold. Soon, tiny ice crystals form an ice skin, on the water surrounding the rock. It is minus 15 degrees below zero, even on this mild spring day, minus 30 with the wind chill. In minutes the lake is a frozen tomb, twice a man's height deep, a cratal mausoleum with massive, near-vertical walls.

But before the ice quite overcomes the rock of the meteorite, the rock shudders and from its bulk, unfolds a monstrous creature. It moves with unearthly nimbleness off the rock and towards the wall of the crater. The water is deep but the devilish form moves underwater with no hindrance. Its red inhuman form battles through the freezing ice, but too late. Already the water is turning solid. Gradually as the demon moves to the wall of the crater it slows; slower and slower it moves until finally it stops. Its efforts have been great but short lived as the ice closes. The thing, imprisoned in a solid prison of ice, calls to its brethren. Even encased in ice, this thing begins to emit a strange, rhythmical pulse.

The Run

"Come on you old bastard", extending an arm to help, I reach down and grab my old Colonel by the scruff of the neck and heave. He kicks his feet at the same time and over he comes, the pair of us land in a heap at the base of the final high wall on the camp's ten klick assault course. I love that moment after a hard work out, you gulp in air and try to get on top of your breathing, it's the most relaxed and peaceful I ever get. I turn around and grin at the Colonel, he grins back, he likes the moment as much as I do.

Me and him go a long way back, he is now a General, big General, but to me, he will always be my Colonel, my mentor, almost a father. I first met him when I joined the Marines, I was literally straight off the street, living from day to day, fight to fight. I had learnt many of the hard lessons of life a long time before: to trust no one, take everything you could and of course the golden rule - those with the gold make all the rules. Finally, it had come down to the stark choice of the armed forces or prison and that is how I ended up in the Marine Corps.

From day one I was in trouble and very quickly gained a reputation as a hard man, a troublemaker but most of all, a loner. I'd had a run-in with a drill sergeant, a bull of a man, he'd taken exception to my marching and kicked the legs from under me, I jumped up and did the same to his face. But a 17-year-old boot neck is no match for a drill sergeant; that evening I was in gaol on a charge and nursing a busted jaw. The following morning, I met the Colonel for the first time. It was very much a one-sided conversation for two reasons, first, even I wasn't stupid enough to answer back to a Colonel and second, talking really hurt my jaw. The company sergeant major had doubled me into the room.

47

"Trooper Lance, Sir!" The last word he practically screamed, like he was addressing the whole regiment.

The Colonel looked me up and down with a poker straight face.

"I'll give it to you straight son", I really hated being called son.

"You think you are tough, you're not", he waved generally in the direction of my face, "not yet at least. You must be the worst recruit we have had in years, you have single-handedly got more charges in one month than the rest of the battalion put together, I'd kick you off but I'd mess up my boots." He looked down at his boots, my gaze followed, they were immaculately polished. "I'd rather tread in dog shit because that's what you are, you are a pile of steaming shit, worse you're the little dung beetle that scurries around in the shit and eats it!" All the time he was becoming redder and redder, I on the other hand, was becoming whiter and whiter. Sure I'd had a few strips torn off me before but not like this, this guy was really scary. He was breathing like a bull before it charges when he suddenly stopped and grinned.

"You know, you remind me of me, I was the exact same self-centred mother fucker that you are. You, my boy, could go far in the marine corp." He glanced down at my papers, though I could tell that he already knew its contents. "Best shot, fittest recruit, best fighter, so what's your problem?" With that, he shut up and waited. Did he expect me to answer? He still waited, I started to panic and after what seemed like an age I replied.

"Er, I" and that was it, he was back.

"I'll tell you what your problem is you have no trust and no loyalty. When you go down in combat and you will, there is only one guy who is going to pick you up and that will be another Marine. We are family and I am just like your Daddy, the one you never had." He again looked down at the papers. "So this is how it shapes up, from today I am promoting you to Lead Cadet. In one month you will be standing back there where you are now, if you've done well you will keep your rank, if you've not, I'll bust your ass and you'll do your entire service smashing rocks.

Dismissed." With that, I was doubled out of his office. I couldn't believe it, the Lead Cadet was always the best and brightest recruit and usually the best brown nose and now it was me. No one had ever given me a break like that before, no one had ever trusted me like that before and from that moment on I never looked back. I owed the Colonel, I owed him big time.

I push myself up on the assault course wall and with exactly the same tone he'd used all those years before, he says.

"I'll not shit you, Lance, I didn't come up here for my health, I want to talk to you."

I jump to my feet, dust off my combats and pull the Colonel up.

"Let's walk."

The two of us do exactly that for a while, he has already let me know it is important so he gives me a chance to get my thoughts together, no doubt while he does the same.

"There is going to be a big show" he starts, "biggest one for a while, as <u>usual</u> they want it done yesterday and the clock is already ticking. All the units are sending their best men, there's going to be <u>thorough</u> selection and the best man gets the job. It's going to be a <u>four man</u> team; you if you get to go, are the muscle."

I look at him, smiling and shaking my head – he must be taking the piss.

"Maybe five years ago, but not now, I am out of shape and remember this!" I slid my T-shirt down off my shoulder, to reveal my bad shrapnel wound.

The reaction is severe, his face contorts in pain, I have not seen him like that since his wife died. "Remember it", he gasps desperately fighting his anger, perhaps he felt responsible for it, which I suppose he was. "Remember it, I sent you on that mission and I got you back out of it, but that last show was nothing, NOTHING! This is possibly the biggest thing you and I will ever do and the last person I want to send is you, you're like my son, but you are also the best and if I say you are up for it, you go!"

Where the hell did that come from, I smile.

"Well, I am glad we sorted that out."

The Rescue

Breakfast was a muted affair after the previous night's drinking. Lazenby and Blenkinsopp had the briefest of whispers as both selected food from the buffet.

"How'd' it go?" asked Blenkinsopp without even looking at Lazenby.

"Not well!"

Lazenby sat down heavily, alone at his table, he was tired and reflected on last night, would he get away with it.

"As long as we get to the States, I'm alright." he said to himself over and over.

He looked out of the port windows and forward at the Sun which had already pulled away from the sea and was beginning to climb in the sky.

"PORT, my God we are going east, back to Germany" he whispered to himself. He had involuntarily clutched at the table and now mentally forced his shoulders to slowly relax and continue to eat his breakfast, though his stomach churned inside.

Just before he had finished his breakfast, a very agitated Captain Eckner entered the room.

"Can I have everybody's attention please" he stated in a voice used to command.

"Ladies and Gentlemen there is no need for any alarm. We have been asked to assist a German research centre in the arctic, they are in difficulties. I assure you that this will have little impact on your journey, but we will arrive some 36 hours late. Our trip could save the lives of the men and I am sure that you will understand."

Then proudly; "The Hindenburg is the only vessel in the world that can rescue these men, as no ship could make it through the pack ice. I hope you will enjoy the trip to the Arctic and I am sure the crew will try to make your extended stay as comfortable as possible, after all, this is a floating first class hotel." He turned to leave and almost as an afterthought:

"We will be meeting a German ship to take on extra personnel to help in the rescue, Thank you." With that, he left.

Immediately the passengers burst into conversation, some excited about the arctic, some were worried about the poor stranded men, others just complained about the delay. Lazenby, relaxed for a moment at least he was off the hook, unless of course, this was another rouse.

Four hours later, just before lunch, the ship approached a German frigate. It was a delicate operation with the Hindenburg approaching into the wind. A miscalculation or a change of wind direction would cause the whole ship to swivel and make picking up men and supplies impossible. The large rope hawsers were dropped close the frigate, whose crew actually made mundane the job of collecting the ropes, tethering them to the winches and pulling the Hindenburg into a controlled station. As both the Frigate steamed and the airship flew into the wind, a winch lowered a line from the bow of the Hindenburg. This was watched avidly by the passengers from the promenade windows and who by craning their necks, got a pretty good view. A significant amount of stores were brought on board, mainly cold climate equipment like furs and snow shoes.

The operation went well until a Hindenburg crew member, trying to keep the nose heavy ship in trim, jettisoned two tonnes of water onto the ship's crew below. Then the whole event took on a more menacing twist when eight well-armed ski troopers came on deck and were hoisted up. Each was dressed in heavy quilted jackets, fur lined forage caps and two carried rifles with scopes, the rest of the soldiers carried machine guns. Judging by their kit these were no ordinary troops. Lazenby noticed their weapons, he had never seen machine guns like the ones these soldiers carried; they were futuristic – like something from Buck Rodgers matinee films. The passengers started to buzz, particularly amongst the British and American passengers.

"Why do they need soldiers, I thought this was a rescue mission," said one.

"Well, who would you send if not soldiers?"

"But why do they need guns?"

"I suppose there are polar bears!"

Lord Rothschild showed unusual insight by saying:

"I want to know what the hell a frigate with ski troops is doing here anyway; we must be just off Norway now, surely."

The conversation continued on this subject for some time, but eventually the passengers went onto other topics and then onto lunch. By the time the Hindenburg cast off from the ship, barely a passenger noticed, except for Lazenby and Blenkinsopp, of course.

Following the rendezvous with the ship, the Hindenburg turned to a northerly course and kept it. The temperature steadily dropped, even inside the heated cabins, though it was not sufficient to make the passengers do more than put on a pullover. For the crew however it was quite different, all of them worked in unheated areas and some were fully in the elements, but the crew worked on cheerfully wearing some of the extra clothing brought on from the ship.

By the following morning the first icebergs were spotted, monumental mountains of ice afloat on the sea; even from altitude they were magnificent. Three hours later, a little before lunch, the Hindenburg crossed overland or rather moved from liquid water to solid water. It was stunning to see the rugged land stretching out as far as the eye could see, but without a single true piece of substance. It had soaring towers, plinths and titanic walls, all of ice. Yet, however insubstantial and impermanent these structures looked, this ice could well have fallen from the skies when Julius Caesar marched his armies across the world and may not finally melt into the ocean for another two millennia – would any of man's creations last longer?

To the passengers this whole event, whilst been initially very exciting, soon faded to a poor third in comparison with the delights of lunch and then the bar. None of the passengers, except perhaps a handful, even contemplated how difficult it would be to stop the Hindenburg and get men onto the ground. There were no winches here, no 100 strong ground crew to leap for the ropes, only a few starving men who were maybe already dead.

Lazenby and Blenkinsopp were at the bar amongst perhaps ten other passengers; both were studiously not associating with each other but were debating with different groups. At around 15:00 the Hindenburg had managed to 'dock' on the ice pack and there was again a good deal of excitement but that was some two hours ago.

Lazenby and a few others, including the writer Charter were listening to Lord Rothschild, a popular passenger, for once without his wife, she had retired with a headache.

"Have you heard, some boffin has come up with the idea of dialling for the police on an Emergency number – 999, can you imagine. I will get an instant response from the "Old Bill" and then I will only have to wait an hour for the sergeant to get on his bike and cycle the five miles to the estate – for God's sake the wife would have already killed me by then!"

The party around him laughed merrily; Rothschild, who was the sort of man with an infectious laugh and a beaming smile, only the most dour of company, could resist his genuine good spirits.

Rothschild suddenly looked very serious and put his finger over his mouth.

"I've got some really interesting news, gather round, you know it's very 'hush hush'."

The group drew closer, so close that they looked as if they were in a rugby scrum. Very quietly he began.

"The steward and I shared a bottle last night, you know ...... it helps pass the time. Anyway, we got pretty friendly, so friendly that when I saw him this morning he was bursting to tell me some news." With that, he looks up and around the room, once sure that none of the crew are in ear shot he continues.

"Seems that Mörder chap was more than just a soldier. Apparently, he is some sort of high priest of this weird Nazi Occult thing, like a grand wizard of a coven, or something like that anyway. Last night he was up to no good in the cargo bay, they say he was trying to summon Satan himself, there is a circle of blood, candles and everything that you might expect, but wait for it, for the only thing there isn't is Mörder. He is not on the ship anymore!"

"What do you mean he is not on the ship, he'll be in his bunk?" said Charter.

"No, No, the crew have looked high and low, he is not aboard."

"He's dead then, he must have fallen or may be jumped," Lazenby added, thinking he should say it before anybody else did.

"Maybe?" Rothschild continued, "But the crew think that something evil has happened to him, they also think that his tricks last night and this trip to the Pole are connected, in short, they think that we are cursed. Yes cursed."

"Poppycock and rubbish, sailors are always a superstitious lot and those on airships must be even worse," said Charters.

"I tell you no good will come of it." Rothschild said whilst vigorously shaking his head.

Lazenby could only add, "Yes, one way or another, it's a bad omen."

Lazenby casually turned to look for Blenkinsopp and was startled to see him standing with a very serious looking Captain Eckner and an ashen faced Kruger. Lazenby, heart momentarily fluttered as he saw Kruger.

Surprisingly, Blenkinsopp was nodding vigorously and then beckoned him across to join them. As he approached he could see Kruger clearly objecting to his inclusion but heard Blenkinsopp say.

"Capital fellow, just come back from Persia, a good chemist, would be very useful."

Captain Eckner proffered a hand.

"Mr. Lazenby, we are er…..experiencing some technical ….challenges, I am getting together what expertise we have on board to try to resolve it"

"Where did you read Chemistry?" Kruger quite rudely interjected.

"Cambridge, under Professor Burrows." Lazenby lied fluently, he had actually read Classics, but his room-mate had read chemistry, so he figured he could wing it.

"Professor Burrows, the plastic expert," nodded Eckner, noticeably impressed.

Again Kruger erupted into the conversation, with venom.

"What were you doing in Persia?"

Again Lazenby was lucky, he had done a posting in Persia flying with the Royal Air Corp, one of his tasks had been aerial photography to map the area and working with British Petroleum, BP. With war looming the British government wanted maps and they wanted oil.

"I was a chemist supporting oil exploration for BP."

Eckner looked at Kruger, who frowned and shook his head. In any other circumstances a German, even a noble German like Captain Eckner would not directly ignore the advice of one so well positioned in the Nazi party; but here Eckner was the concerned captain of a ship and he still made the decisions.

"Gentlemen, follow me."

The four men went down onto B Deck and followed the route taken the previous night by Lazenby. As they stopped momentarily to enter the cargo hold, Lazenby noticed that the door to the hangar was chained and a hand written note "Verboten" was stuck to the door. Despite himself, Lazenby looked into Kruger's coal black eyes, both men had completely blank expressions, Lazenby looked away – would Kruger make something of this?

As they entered the cargo all their eyes were drawn to the floor. For in the large open space in front of the davit was scrawled a pentagon surrounded by a circle with strange hieroglyphs around it. Lying on a packing crate, now closed with its clasp firmly locked, was the 'Key of Solomon'. Lazenby almost choked as he saw the book, he realised that in his haste after killing Mörder, he had just left the book. He thought how odd it was, that the quarry of his mission, lay there within reach, but just as unobtainable as ever, for the moment at least. It did not look or feel like the book from last night, the evil aura was not there, it looked no more than a very old book.

Captain Eckner was not happy, "I thought I told you to clean that filth off my deck!" he blasted at the unsuspected davit operator.

"Er, no sir!" The junior hand mumbled. He had not been told to clean it up, but he could see the gathering cloud on Eckner's face, then realized his error, "Er, Yes sir, immediately."

Griegmiers, the executive officer, who was supervising the winch, stepped in to help the hapless crewmember.

"Sir, I ordered some of the crew to attend to it, but we have more urgent tasks at hand." He paused for a moment, in doubt whether he should go on, then decided to plunge in, "Er, frankly sir, the crew feel uncomfortable with it, I think they'd rather clean the heads."

Captain Eckner threw him a withering look, but Griegmiers stood firm, as Executive Officer it was his job to keep the Captain informed of the mood of the crew, even if it meant a verbal lashing.

"Griegmiers, the crew don't get paid to think, that's your job, so why don't you start"

"Yes, sir"

Eckner, still not satisfied turned his attention to Kruger and gave him an equally filthy look which spoke volumes for his hatred of the Nazi occultists. Lazenby noticed that Kruger had now also spotted the Grimoire lying on the crate. Lazenby allowed himself a small smile, for Kruger had to feign disinterest, just as he did.

The poor junior hand passed to each of them heavy fur coats, hats and mittens, they then climbed into the basket under the davit and with a short order from Eckner, they started to descend. In a moment they were clear of the ship, the weather was clear with only the hint of a wind.

"We were lucky with the weather, even a five mile an hour wind and we could not have landed the men." Eckner said.

Within moments they were on the snow. Tracks led off in the direction that the ship was facing, in the distance, they could see people at work in front of a large ice drift. From no point other than the gondola, could anyone on the ship see this.

"I commend you on your navigation captain, I did not notice any change in direction coming, but here you are right on the nail." Blenkinsopp said grinning.

Contrary to all expectation Eckner looked uncomfortable with this description and moved on at a faster pace.

As they came closer they could see activity, a few crew members and the soldiers busying themselves, moving up and down the guide rope which clung to the side of the very steep snow drift. A small tent nestled at the base of the drift, large enough for 10 men to sleep in, but certainly not a research base; Blenkinsopp was starting to become very unhappy.

"I am starting to smell a rat, gentlemen. This ain't no base, this ain't no rescue mission – what the hell is going on here?"

By now they were nearing the tent.

"Please, step inside gentlemen" pleaded Eckner.

Blenkinsopp, now thoroughly distrusting stopped at the entrance, looked meaningfully at the other men, but saved a particularly withering stare for Kruger and then entered.

Inside the tent was warm and well lit. Drinking tea at a makeshift table was another one of the passengers, neither Lazenby nor Blenkinsopp knew him. Behind him stood a statuesque lieutenant dressed in heavy furs, his automatic weapon swinging by his side.

Eckner stepped forward and announced them,

"Can I introduce Mr. Blenkinsopp, an American engineer and Mr. Lazenby a British chemist." Then turning around and motioning his hand towards the man drinking tea.

"This is the most esteemed Professor Karl Von Weingang"

Lazenby almost blurted out,

"What, the Egyptologist!" then recovering a little he offered his hand "it's an honour, Sir." After all, Lazenby had a keen interest in the classics and history and it is not every day you meet an esteemed Egyptologist in the Arctic Circle.

"And this," continued Eckner, "is Lieutenant Schumann, the leader of the ski troops attached to us."

Schumann nodded and crisply clicked his heels together, though his steel grey eyes never left Lazenby.

"Hold it guys," an annoyed Blenkinsopp broke in, "this is all very cosy fellows, but what the hell is going on here!"

Eckner looked at the other men.

"This is a delicate matter and before I tell you any more, I will need your word as gentlemen that you will not discuss this with anybody else," then with meaning, "ever!"

They all nodded their ascent.

"Yesterday at around 4am, Germany's most powerful radio station started picking up interference. It was relatively strong and so it was assumed to be a problem with the equipment. It initially, seemed to random pulses, but one of the radio operators noticed that it was actually a pattern, 1, 3, 5, 7, 11, 13, 17, 19. This would then repeat itself."

Lazenby and Blenkinsopp were nodding their understanding, both fascinated.

"I may be a brilliant Egyptologist, but I am no mathematician, can someone explain."

Blenkinsopp looked at the Professor.

"These are prime numbers, which is to say, a number which can only be divided by itself and one. These could not be random and therefore someone must have been broadcasting the message – it could not have been a fault." He explained

"Exactly Mr. Blenkinsopp", said Eckner, then continued:

"It was not a fault but a transmission. The radio station estimated that it must be no more than 50 miles away, with the power of the signal, even their equipment could not have broadcast further than 100 miles" He paused for a moment.

"Imagine the surprise, gentlemen, when they discovered that every single radio set in Germany was picking up the same transmission and that even our embassies around the world were also receiving it."

Again the Professor sort some clarification,

"But you said that the source was only 50 miles away from the first radio station; how can that be?"

Eckner looked slowly at everybody around the room.

"Using triangulation, we pinpointed the transmitter's position to the North Pole, right here where we are. Whatever it is that is transmitting it doing so at 1000 times the strength of anything that we have on earth!"

The Prisoner

Unknown location; with Major Lance.

"What's your name?"

PAIN

"Fuck off!" I say through gritted teeth.

MORE PAIN

"When I get out of here; I am going fuck you up!" I shout this time, or maybe scream, I am starting to lose it.

INTENSE PAIN

This time, I have no words, just grunts. I have a Hessian bag over my head, I can't see my protagonists, I can barely hear them, over my own noise. They have kindly soaked the bag first, I am struggling to breathe. Whoever it was has decided to stick his fingers into my, not yet healed, shrapnel wound.

OUTLANDISH PAIN........BLACK......

Thud! A punch in the face, not nice when you can't even see it coming but at least it brings me back round. It's not so much the pain of the punch, it is the anticipation of the next one that scares you.

"Huh!" another strike, where else? My bollocks.

All I can think is that it has to be over; they can't kill me, can they? For god's sake, it's only a test, they're on my side! I have done these tests before, but never like this.

The Colonel had promised a pretty intense selection process for the job. I was confident, over the years I had been on this type of selection course four or five times. It had started as you would expect, an assault course, a log run, a high assault course. A ferocious 30 km mountainous night tab with full kit and some complex navigation. Then, with no sleep, straight onto the shooting, CQB (close quarter battle), long range sniper style shooting and then live fire in the killing rooms, point blank, fast reaction stuff. More tabbing, no sleep, problem-solving, more tabbing, assault course, no sleep. Three days constant and while it was the hardest I had ever been pushed, it was still the usual.

The selection, at least from what I had seen, had lost ninety percent and we were now down to the last twenty. Quite a few looked in much better shape than I did. We were all gathered next to a series of bunkers, then one by one, we were lead off round back of the complex.

I was greeted by one of the military's favourites, the underwater pipe crawl. It was a pipe an arm's length wide, full of water. Normally, the pipe is not much longer than it is wide. Deep breath, push your legs, pull with your arms and you are out. This, this was different. I was standing in front of a small grass bank, I couldn't see over the top of it, but the pipe must have been at least 10 paces long – that's fucking scary. I was standing there, a physical shambles, I was thinking that this was borderline, as to whether I could get through.

A squaddie wearing a balaclava to cover his face, barked,

"Deep breath and crack on."

Pointlessly I asked, "How Far?"

He shrugged, "Crack on!"

I took ten deep breaths and tried to oxygenate my blood then plunged in. Luckily I was already freezing cold so the freezing water had less impact than normal; but I still immediately got really bad 'ice-cream head', but I pushed on into the dark, water-filled pipe.

Fear is a killer here. Fear causes your heart to beat faster, which in turn burns your air.

"Stay calm." I heard my inner voice say and I listened to it. I started crawling forward in controlled but quick movements. I was counting, each time I moved my left knee. I was trying to work out how many I needed to get through, I reckoned about ten.

Five steps. Good, I reckoned halfway.

Ten steps. Nearly there, should have seen some light or something.

Fifteen. Nothing. Fuck, how far was this?

Twenty. Doubt was pushing at the back of my mind.

Twenty Four. My lungs heaved for the first time. Holy shit! This was getting close.

Twenty Six. Fear clutched at me, drowning was not the way I had planned to die. I could hear the blood banging in my ears as my heart pumped.

Twenty Seven. The air I was holding bursts from my lung, but I forced myself not to breath.

Twenty Eight. Fuck, Shit, Twat!

Twenty something. I gasped a mouth full of water. I was losing consciousness......

I opened my eyes and wretched water. I was lying on my back so I rolled over onto all fours; puked and snorted about a pint of water. As I got my breath, I looked up at a soldier; this time without the balaclavas on.

"Are you fucking kidding!" I gasped.

This is way beyond anything I had ever experienced on selection course.

He helped me up onto my feet.

"Well done mate, you've passed. Here's a brew."

He pushed a large cup into my hand, I took a gulp, it was sweet and hot. It's amazing what a brew can do for your morale.

He pointed at a small shed.

"Just step in there mate and we can complete your paperwork, then you get well-deserved rest." He beamed enthusiastically.

I wandered over to shed; but I have played this game before! This was back to the normal drill, they tell you that you are done and see if you switch off. As I stepped through the door four big marines jump me, they want to know if I could go the extra yard. Well, a couple of those marines won't go the extra yard, at least not without crutches. I managed to give them the slip and got on with the last phase, the E&E (escape and evasion). After, about eight hours they found me. Then the whole squad had a go, to square away what I had done to their friends. I was a mess by the end of that and it's been downhill since.

"Look, tell us your name and it's all over." Whispering in my left ear.

"We know your name anyway, we just want you to tell us." Another voice in my right ear. When they put me in the chair they tied my arms and legs down to the seat – but not my head. Payback, I whip my head round as fast as I can. Crunch. It hurts like hell but I have the satisfaction of feeling his teeth smash against my forehead. He steps back screaming. Unfortunately, my movement had unbalanced the chair, I fall forward, face smashing into the deck.

"Give him a good fucking hiding."

I lay there dazed, now I know I am going to die. Like the start of a summer shower, the first boot lands, a noticeable pause, then another followed almost immediately by another, then the heavens open.

PAIN

I can't breathe, am I dying….., I can't breathe if I could speak I would say my name, I can't breathe, Oh God!

BLACK.

The Thing

Ice Cap, March 1937, Wednesday 15:00 hrs.

One of the crew, heavily covered in furs, entered the tent where the "experts" were waiting huddled around a small but surprisingly warm paraffin heater. Eckner was talking and in the crew man's enthusiasm he blurted out his message.

"Mr. Griegmiers' compliments, Sir, we are almost through."

A pain flickered across Eckner's face and he shot a black look at the man. Eckner, was a gentleman, a lord even, his generation were always calm under fire, never rushed, always composed. He would happily stand on the bridge of his ship as it went down in flames. The crew man's excitement drained visibly from his face and he said stupidly:

"Err… Sorry, Sir," and left.

Each man in the room was equally excited by the news. These men represented some of the most forward-thinking minds of their age, but each also remembered that he was a gentleman.

"As I was saying," continued Eckner, "We assume that this thing, whatever it is, must have dropped from the sky, burning red hot and hit the ice cap. The impact created a large crater but the great residual heat of the object melted the surrounding ice, creating a great pool of water. This, inevitably, cooled and turned back to ice. This object, animal or mineral, is encased in ice, which we are now cutting and melting. There are two interesting points – the 'thing' seems to have moved away from the rock and it also seems that its transmitter is so powerful, it is completely swamping all our communications."

"No communication, so we are on our own?" asked Blenkinsopp. Eckner nodded looking meaningfully at each of the men. Lazenby was the only man there who was actually relieved by the fact.

And then, as if the crewman had just entered:

"Ah, it seems as though we are nearly ready, would you follow me."

The six men, Lazenby, Blenkinsopp, Eckner, the Professor, Kruger and Schumann moved back outside into the clear but freezing day of the polar ice cap.

Each, in turn, grabbed the guide rope that moved up the snow drift, which was as high as a house. It was difficult going as the ice was surprisingly solid and slippery. Blenkinsopp stumbled twice but on both occasions, he was grabbed by the Lieutenant, who seemed to pick him up and put him back on the rope, as if Blenkinsopp were no more than a child.

As each man cleared the summit they let out an audible gasp. In front of them lay a stadium of Olympian proportions. It looked like a dormant volcano with steep sides and a perfectly flat bottom which from the top looked like a lake. But its proportions were monumental, larger than the Circus Maximus, larger than any football or baseball stadium.

In the middle of this epic stadium small ant-like figures could be seen working. The team quickly descended on a guide rope and moved quickly to their goal. About 10 of the ship's crew were working hard, whilst the troopers were standing guard. Supervising the men in their work was the young Eckner, whose mountain experience was a huge asset. The crew had erected a large stanchion, from which a thick rope had been lowered, they were exerting themselves, pulling a large object, covered in a tarpaulin up from the pit below. The block was the size of a motor vehicle and much to everybody's disappointment, nothing could be seen of the contents. The crew swung around and lowered the object onto the solid ice cap, a senior hand ran forward, leapt up on top and began to undo the ropes. With a quick glance at Eckner to confirm his next action, he let the tarpaulin go.

There was an audible gasp from the men; only the handful of men working on cutting this object out had seen it, for everybody else, this was the first and a most shocking glimpse. A few of the crew crossed themselves and muttered prayers. Lazenby distinctly heard the words: Satan, Devil, Evil and most interestingly the name of Mörder. The ice casing glistened and was crystal clear, as the crew had melted the last of the ice to rescue the object. Inside this ice tomb was an horrific scorpion like creature. Its torso was both the shape and size of a coffin, it had six legs, its tail curved back over its body ending in a wicked sting, it was faceless. But by far the most striking feature were two fearfully powerful claws, which were large enough to go around a man's waist and certainly strong enough to cut that man in two. Its colour was difficult to gauge, encased as it was in shining ice and with the low fairy sun of the pole, it was certainly a crimson red colour but also seemed to be implausibly shiny, even metallic, like the chitin shell of a beetle.

The stunned silence was shattered as the sting of the tail, pulsed a bright, deep red. The action itself was silent, but immediately caused panic amongst the crew who hurriedly dived for cover, ran, swore, one clearly wet himself – a particularly bad idea in this climate. Some, however, did not move, the six gentlemen and the lieutenant, whilst his highly trained troops' only action was to raise their weapons and point it at the beast.

"Stand firm," ordered Eckner, his voice carried weight, all men stood still.

"Look" pointed Blenkinsopp excitedly, "three pulses, I would wager the next one will be five."

Sure enough, after the three pulses were five, then seven, then eleven.

"It must be part of the transmission device," said the Professor.

Eckner turned and looked at the group,

"I have only these questions, is it animal or machine? Is it from this planet? But most of all is it safe to put on my ship? If it is not, then I will throw it back into that hole."

Lazenby moved forward, swooped down to pick up a hammer from the crews' equipment and moved to the object.

"Look, part of the claw is sticking out of the ice"

With that he gave the claw a healthy tap with the hammer and to everyone's genuine relief, a loud metallic clang rang out.

"I'd say it was a machine and if it's a machine somebody has made it and if somebody can make it, we can certainly break it." Lazenby said this with a smug smile on his lips but also with confidence. It had the desired effect, though he himself did not believe a word of it. To the crew it had moved quickly from being the spawn of hell, bringing the end of the earth, to a mechanical device, however impressive, most of these men were engineers, they understood mechanics, they did not understand theology or mythology. Lazenby, on the other hand just knew that this was important, too important to be lost, better on a German airship that must fly over England than lost to the polar ice cap.

Blenkinsopp took his lead from Lazenby.

"Nothing, even if it was still alive or should I say operative could break out of that ice, I would say that it is safe."

Eckner looked next to the Professor for his comment.

"As you know I am an historian, not an engineer, a fact to me is not black and white, true of false but something that needs to be interpreted so that it can fit into the greater jigsaw puzzle. This 'thing' looks like a creature, you say it is metal, well maybe where this comes from all creatures are metal. If it is manufactured, I for one, have never seen its like before; we stand here under one of the marvels of our modern science, The Hindenburg and yet this looks centuries ahead of our technology. How therefore, can we gauge its capabilities, I say it is alien, I say dangerous but I too say we must put it aboard – I have unearthed Egyptian kings, mummified next to golden chariots but this makes my life work look mundane."

Finally, Eckner looked at the Nazi Kruger for his words.

"The scorpion is a powerful creature, you can freeze them like this in ice, then use a blow torch to melt the ice and the scorpion will walk away undamaged. They say that if a disaster were to kill all life on earth, the scorpion would be the last creature to die. God has delivered this weapon to the Third Reich, we should use it."

"Jesus!" Lazenby muttered under his breath if there were many more like Kruger in Germany, then a war would come, sooner rather than later.

Eckner noticeably ignored his son and asked for no advice, he just said;

"You have all given me your answers, though they contradict each other, all of you say we should take this object back to Germany. Remember while we carry this thing, our radio will not work, we will truly be alone; even the normal ship's operations become difficult without a radio."

He turned to his crew and in a loud commanding voice ordered

"Get it on board, we will soon lose the light."

The crew made surprisingly short work of moving the scorpion across the perfectly flat bottom of the crater, then up and down the walls; finally, it was hoisted into the cargo bay. As the creature was being lifted, some of the ship's crew had their first chance of a rest for some hours. They mumbled between themselves, Lazenby was in earshot but this either did not bother them or perhaps they thought his German was not that good.

"I could kill a cigarette. Hans, I tell you no good will come of this. I don't like it. Witchcraft and monsters have no place on our ship."

"Yeah, I told you Jan that Mörder was one of those crazy Nazi priests, but you didn't believe. I tell you he has summoned the very devil into the world."

"Has anybody seen Mörder, I was talking to some of the lads and they reckon he jumped, some even say that the Satan took him, I thought they were talking bollocks till I saw that thing, now I am not so sure."

"Yeah, either way, I will be glad to get home and get that Devil's spawn off the ship"

"Aye Aye to that."

At that moment the ice-encrusted monster disappeared into the hull of the ship and the winch brake was applied.

The crew started to clear away for take-off. After a minute the cage was lowered again and Lazenby joined the rest of the gentlemen and officers to be winched up.

As they boarded the cage no one spoke, they were all deep in their thoughts, whether it was of the crews' safety, of xenology, theology or even mythology, each had his own perception of the recent events. Lazenby cast his eyes around, he considered how odd it was to have visited the North Pole for these last few hours. It was something he would never forget; being a pragmatist he doubted he would ever return. As the gentlemen's' head cleared the deck of the ship, Lazenby noticed something very quickly.

"Captain," he said, "was it your intention to put the creature inside the circle?"

All eyes immediately turned to the floor. Unwittingly, the crew had placed the scorpion in the biggest open space in the cargo bay, but by coincidence, it was exactly in the middle of the circle, which was still painted on the floor. This shook an already nervous crew. One lost his control and flew from the room, screaming.

Eckner took control. "Everybody out, lock the door and lieutenant I want one of your men guarding this thing 24 hours a day.

Within another hour the Hindenburg was heading south, back to Germany.

At dinner that evening Eckner announced very casually that the stranded expedition had managed to walk to another base and was out of any danger. Lazenby thought that this was a clever strategy because it effectively became a non-story, even the passengers would see this detour as nothing more than a short interruption to cruise. Eckner finished his speech by telling the passengers that they had left extra supplies for the men and with compliments of the passengers of the Hindenburg, a crate of Napoleon brandy. This was greeted with a warm applause. As dinner was nearly completed the steward came over to first Lazenby, then Blenkinsopp and the professor to invite them to join Eckner for a smoke. Moments later Eckner rose to his feet and the men all made their way to the staircase leading to B deck.

Eckner greeted the men warmly, though he was positively frosty when Kruger appeared:

"I thought I'd join you for a smoke."

The five men headed for the smoke room but instead entered the main service corridor and headed to the stern of the ship, where the "scorpion" had been stored.

Halfway down the corridor, the group met Schumann, his heels snapped together as the group approached.

"Anything to report Schumann," the Captain asked.

"No Sir, I checked no more than ten minutes ago."

The grouped walked on down the corridor, casually; they were what they were, a group of gentlemen taking their constitutional after a large meal. They were at ease and no one would imagine that they were going to inspect a cursed, demonic spawn, creature.

Lazenby turned to Schumann who had tagged on the end of the group.

"That's a fine weapon you have there, what do you call it?"

He nodded his head to the automatic weapon slung over Schumann's shoulder.

Schumann took the weapon from his back and caressed it like you might a pet cat. It was what would later be known as the MP40 or to most the Schmeisser, but this was a prototype of the MP38. It was sleek and thoroughly modern looking, all made of dark grey metal, with a folding metal stock. To Lazenby it looked like something that a comic book alien would carry, it was striking.

"This Mr. Lazenby is an example of German ingenuity and engineering prowess. This Sir will be the German army's new machine gun if we had enough of these in the First World War, we would not have lost."

"Ah, I think you will find it is the soldier behind the gun; that makes the difference."

"Quite right Mr. Lazenby but good soldiers with good weapons, beat good soldiers with bad weapons. A weapon like this will make the French defences obsolete, these are mobile weapons for a mobile war, not trench warfare"

"You, mean the Maginot line, the impregnable Maginot line, a line of gun emplacements, bunkers and underground barracks that runs half the length of France. And you think that this gun will defeat that?"

"The French are going to fight a war that is 20 years out of date and it will not just be this weapon, we have many new weapons in Germany"

"And how long before you use your new weapons on Britain?" Lazenby asked.

"Most of the wars in Europe, we have both been fighting against France, after all, the Angles and the Saxons are German people. Even our language is the same, how much does the 'Vater land' sound like the English Father Land."

Lazenby desperately tried to keep a straight face, of all the words to choose; why did Schumann choose that one. The rest of the group did not respond, even Blenkinsopp, apparently the verb "to fart" had not reached his neighbourhood yet. Covering his mouth with his hand in a mock yawn Lazenby changed the subject back to the gun.

"Yes, it looks very impressive, but I am keen on guns and hunting and I never saw anything like that before."

Schumann's pride momentarily faded, "Ah yes, it is yet on trial; arctic trial to be precise."

"Secret trial!" Kruger broke in, "So maybe you will stop telling Mr. Lazenby all of it capabilities."

"Yes Sir", said a now sheepish Schumann, "I will go and check on my troops," and with that, he moved back up the corridor.

Eckner was leading the group, as he neared the door he was saying,

"Of course, we have a man on guard for every watch, keeping an eye on our little friend, though I don't expect any trouble with it being encased in…"

Mid-sentence he swung the door open, his last word stuck in his throat, as the group surveyed the room.

"Ice…."

Where the creature had been encased in ice lay the shattered remains of its tomb, large irregular blocks of ice scattered across the floor. Many of these blocks were rose tinted, the reason not being immediately obvious, until the men noticed a broad red stain leading from the inside the pentagon, across the surrounding circle and disappearing behind a row of crates.

The Swarm

The Void.

Utter blackness, frozen, nothing, the Void. Then God said "Let there be light" and behold there was light; but this was not a light burning with a celestial warmth, this was a spiralling, white hot, desolate flame. It stood there like a gaping wound, in the fabric of space, pulsating as if driven by a heartbeat within. Then slowly a black cloud moved towards the flame, blacker than the blackness of space. It crept towards the light, like a cancerous growth. As the amorphous cloud came closer it could be seen that its immeasurable depth of darkness was made from innumerable specs, each fated to spiral towards the light. Slowly the dots came closer, irregular blocks of once molten rock, the very stuff of the universe, all shapes, all sizes. Some no larger than a small house, others the size of small moons, all tumbling as if choreographed in the most complex cosmic ballet. But as they came closer still, each seemed to sprout arachnid legs and scorpion tail, for each carried its deadly parasitic monster. On each and every one of the million rocks clung a demonic form, destined to infest the universe. A million monsters falling into the oblivion of the light. Like the vanquished angels who fell defeated from heaven to hell, they were legion, ten score by ten score by ten score. They were a Swarm.

The first rock reached the light, a bright flash as it crashed into the centre of the cosmic whirlpool and was gone. Summoned across the dimensions by a voice, by many voices. These flashes, at first regular like a lighthouse, then a strobe, but quickly built to a crescendo of continuous light, as each rock bearing spawn impacted the heart. Still, nine days, as man would mark time before the last devilish light illuminated the void.

The whirlpool of fire pulsed a moment longer, then collapsed upon itself, as if the fire had consumed itself. The next moment it was gone as if it had never existed.

The Team

Unknown hospital facility with Major Lance.

I was having a nice dream that involved three women, when one of them starting shaking me and it hurt, so I woke up.

"Come on sleepy head", says an extremely attractive young nurse, actually prettier than the ones I was dreaming about, "You've got a visitor."

I try to push myself up the bed using my elbows – it hurts – like hell, but I manage it. The nurse fusses over me, puffing up my pillows and generally being nice to me, so I cannot see the visitor, though I'm not complaining.

I see a hand slip over her shoulder and pull her away.

"He's a war veteran mam, he'll manage." It's the Colonel.

"Who the fuck were those Muppets and what the hell have you got me into." I am not very happy with him, worse, when I have my little outburst, I realise some of my ribs are broken – ouch.

"AND, how in God's name am I meant to go on your mission; when I am in this state?"

He just smiles at me and plays to my not considerable ego.

"Outstanding! I told them you were the man, 3,000 of the best we had and an old bastard, a wounded old bastard, came through with the goods."

Okay, that sounds a bit better, nice to know that I am valued.

"Tomorrow," he says, "you will thank me, you've done all the hard work, one small task to do and you will be the biggest hero – ever!"

Biggest, Hero and Ever; these were the sort of words I definitely wanted to hear, I had no idea what the hell he was talking about, but it sounded good.

"It's time to meet the team; come on get your kit on."

"THE team, don't you mean MY team." I quiz him, the Colonel was always very specific with his words.

"Sorry, you're not running this show."

That was worth leaping out of bed for, every mission I had worked on with the Colonel I had led, I am now very angry. Unfortunately, I'd not realised I was stark bollock naked and I have always found it difficult to be aggressive, whilst hiding my genitals behind my hands.

"Don't get uppity, this is not a military job, it's scientific, they're leading it." He smiles at me again. "I told you, you're just the hired muscle. Come on they are just out here." He starts through the door turns and says smiling rakishly "Oh, by the way, your boss is a woman" and then he's gone.

Blaspheming fluently, I put on a hospital gown and with my ass showing out of the back, take off after the Colonel. I catch up with him, painfully, half way down the corridor. By now my stunning intellect has got over the issue of serving under a woman and moved on to a more important subject.

"Is she a babe?"

"Not yet," is his rather odd answer.

I must be a sight, half limping, half skipping to keep up with the Colonel and all the time with my butt protruding out from one of those ludicrous, hospital gowns. I follow him through what seems to be a maze of corridors, then finally, he stops at a door, winks at me and enters the room. I bowl in directly after him.

It is like one of those nightmares you have, the one when you wake up naked in the middle of town or at work. I walk into a party, it is not quite 'black tie' but it is not far off. The room is filled with elegant people nibbling on a finger buffet and drinking cocktails. I, on the other hand, am unshaven, all beat up, with my butt hanging out. As I enter, the entire party turns and greets me with a warm applause, I back up to the nearest wall. The Colonel, with his best schmoozing voice on, introduces me.

"Ladies and gentlemen, can I introduce to you a war veteran, a man that has personally saved my life three times. As a soldier he is outstanding, being the most decorated marine in the service, he has served in every significant military action in the last 20 years both as a regular and black ops. He has just competed against 3,000 other troops to earn the right to go on this mission and frankly, he left the rest for dead. He is simply the best I have ever worked with. I give you Major Lance."

This time a more enthusiastic applause and I have to say I am beginning to enjoy this. After the applause dies down, he looks at me.

"Let's step next door and you can meet the team." The Colonel nods at a group of three people who get up and go into a small side room, I think to myself

"God, let that not be my team."

They are an odd bunch, a petite old women well into her sixties, a quite muscular middle-aged woman, perhaps fifty something and a one-armed man of at least late fifty. They may have made a pretty good bridge team, but that was it, my team must already be in the room.

The Colonel makes straight for the side room, I skirt around the wall, trying to keep the small garment I am wearing between me and the crowd. With a deft move, I even manage to close the door without turning my back to anyone. As I shuffle into the room there are only five occupants, including me.

The Colonel launches in pointing first at the old lady;

"Dr. Moon, Physicist and leader of the expedition"

She steps forward and shakes my hand warmly,

"Major, welcome, we will all feel safer knowing we have you with us," I numbly shake her hand back. She had once been a very attractive woman, even in her sixties she is still striking. She has hazel eyes and olive skin, her long hair is now grey, but I bet it was once dark.

The Colonel moves on next to the one-armed man;

"Lazlo Wolf, hunter and survival expert." The thought crosses my mind that he can't be that good of a survivor if he has lost an arm. He steps forward and shakes with his left hand; he has a grip that could strangle a bear.

"Major, you and I must work together to keep the team alive." For a moment he looks me straight in the eye, whatever he was looking for, he finds, nods at me in satisfaction and steps back. I am also a pretty good judge of character – you could depend on this man.

"Finally," says the Colonel, "Professor Cross, majors in biology and psychology." Again, another beautiful woman that is well past her sell-by date. She steps forward and more caresses my hand than shakes it; she says almost seductively,

"I am looking forward to getting to know you better."

As she steps back I can only shake my head in total disbelief, what the hell was the mission: serve dinner for four people, go for a stroll in the park, catch some public transport – because that is all that this lot were good for.

Dr. Moon senses my confusion, "What is it, Major?"

By now I have had enough, I look at them all one by one, then start my joke:

"A priest, a cripple and nymphomaniac walk into a bar. The barman turns to them and says, 'Is this some kind of joke'?"

At that I theatrically fall about laughing, no one else seems quite so amused. When I finally get control of myself, which was not too long – laughing with broken ribs really hurts; Dr. Moon puts a hand on my shoulder and whilst still looking at me says;

"What have you told him, Colonel, about the mission?"

"Nothing,"

"So he thinks we're all going like this!" It is their turn to laugh, all except Professor Cross who asks, with a very concerned look on her face,

"Was I the nymphomaniac?"

I stay with the team for an hour and we are all fully briefed, apparently even at this late stage only Dr. Moon knew all the facts. As for Cross, Wolf and me, this was the first time that it has really been explained.

After the brief we have a chance to grab a quick drink, the others naturally group together, I stand apart with the Colonel, I want to ask him some questions.

"You picked the team, is there anything I need to know about them?"

"Not really, just trust my judgement, the four of you are literally the best we have, two outstanding scientists, a hunter and of course a...."

"A Killer." I finish his sentence.

He looks at me, shaking his head, "A Soldier, who knows what duty and loyalty mean. You know I have always been proud of you, but this really is the big one. Of all the team, I am most sure of you."

"Thanks. But tell me, something has been worrying me, if Wolf is so good, how come he only has one arm, surely there are plenty of two armed hunters around?"

"Ah yes, Lazlo's arm. It's probably because he only has one arm that we picked him, let me tell you how he lost his arm, better yet..." He waves Wolf over. "Lazlo, Lance here was wondering how you lost your arm?"

I look embarrassingly towards Wolf who as soon as his arm in mentioned subconsciously rubs his stump. His face cracks open into a broad smile.

"Sure it's a good story, not my best, but it's a good one." This guy is obviously a good entertainer, he sets himself up, I'm sure he must have told this story a thousand times.

"I know we are short of time so I'll give you the quick one." He winks at Professor Cross, she smiles coyly, he takes a breath and lunges in. "I'd hit hard times, there was yet another border skirmish, this time a big one and not surprisingly tourist hunters were few on the ground even with my considerable reputation." He smiles disarmingly, even when he was boasting you weren't sure if he was serious.

"I'd had a lean year. Then from out of the blue, four guys turned up asking for a guide, they stunk of drugs, of power and of corruption. My normally fine sense of knowing when to bail out was dulled by the excessive amount of money they wanted to give me. It's amazing how you can convince yourself that wrong is right and right is wrong when there is enough money on the table. Anyway, we had a couple of days hunting. We were stopped a few times by guerrillas, or freedom fighters depending which side you are on, but they knew me and let us pass. Anyway, as was usual we pulled into a small village to re-provision.

It was a virtual war zone, being one of the main guerrilla bases in the area, but again, they knew me and knew me to be honourable, so they let us be. I'd warned the men I was guiding, not to go off, this was a really dangerous place for strangers. Anyway, as sure as night follows day, an hour later they had gone, I had no idea where.

Now, to be honest, I really didn't like these guys, but it's bad form to let your party get murdered so I went after them." He pauses for breath and for the tension to build. "After going down the third side road I found them, they were in a Mexican stand-off with one of the guerrillas. Shit! I thought. I bowled in trying to calm it all down." With this Wolf is bowling across the floor for real, he is acting every last action, he starts to explain where everyone is pointing as he does it.

"So behind me are the four guys of my party, weapons up, one of them has a young kid in a headlock, a pistol pushed to his head. Now I had an alarm bell ringing then, we'd not brought any pistols, not standard kit on hunting and this was a real serious bit of kit, not an old provincial pistol, this was state of the art. Still, I had this focus, they were my responsibility and I had to help them.

Opposite them stands, who else, but the main guerrilla boss, I knew him. Now I am struggling to make out what his angle is, he's got four men, three with guns on him and THEY are the ones scared. Then I see it. In his hand he's got a clacker," he turns to the two women, "it's an er, you know like a switch, a trigger, but these are like a dead man's switch, they go off when you let go of them. Anyway. Sure enough, there's a wire, I follow it and there she is, a landmine and the four guys are practically stood on top of it."

Another pause, he looks around letting the scene sink in. "What are we going to do now? On the one hand, the four guys with guns pointed, one of them at a kid's head, on the other hand, one guy with a land mine. If he fires it he kills the kid and in the middle of all this, yours truly. We all stand there for a minute sweating, thinking how we are going to get out of 'this'. Suddeny, the guerrilla shouts to me 'Hey Wolf, these bastards have my son, you'll pay for bringing them here!' Great, I thought, now I'm getting the blame. So I say 'look guys, I have an idea' and I told them what it was. The guerrilla took some persuading, but he knew my word was good, everybody on the border knows that. We agreed the plan.

I walked over and picked up the landmine - talk about 'putting your head in the jaws of death'. I picked it up and walk away from the group. The idea was simple, both sides trusted me so I put myself up as collateral, anyone tried anything; I'd get blown up, but nobody had a problem with me.

I got to the end of the wire, about as far as I could go and turned around beaming, I'd done it again, tonight I'd be a hero. Sadly, not everyone had read the script, the guy with the pistol slowly lowered his hand, then suddenly lifted and fired at the guerrilla. I turned to the guerrilla, I was sure he'd missed, there was no reaction, then a single drop of blood slid from his forehead to his nose and he dropped down dead."

"There I am holding a land mine that is about to go off. It's funny, but that split second I remember like no other. I could hear my heart beat, ONE, I can still smell all the smells", he sniffs the air for effect. "I can almost taste the air, I can see the guy with the pistol he's smiling, I hear my heart beat, TWO. I can see the boy tearing the arm off him and running sobbing to his dead father, I can see the landmine in my hand, I foolishly realised that I am still smiling, THREE. It dawns on me that these guys are hit-men, they've used me to get them here. This is no accident, this is a 'Hit' and I brought them here, FOUR."

He is standing there, his one half arm stuck out, with his imaginary hand holding the imaginary bomb, his audience is captivated, he waits. There is a tension in the air and he delivers his line with beautiful timing.

"I never heard FIVE."

The women were beside themselves, "What happened? What happened next?" They practically scream.

His shoulders relax, we relax with him. "I woke up hours later all alone. In that split second I saw a rabbit burrow, I stuck the bomb and arm in there. Neither came out again, but it saved my life!" He was chuckling, he enjoyed his own story as much as the rest of us and still chuckling he went off to refill his drink.

I turn to the Colonel, he's nodding his head with one of those really bad, 'I told you so' looks on his face. I shrug, I'll give him this one, Wolf was all I could wish for in a partner.

The Colonel was not through though, he beckons me closer with a tiny shake of his head and whispers the conclusion of the story.

"What he does not tell you is that three months later, those four guys were assassinated. The official report says the shots must have been 1000 paces plus and with a crosswind. How many guys do you think could make that shot?" He turned to walk away, but he had a little bit more, "Oh and the boy in the story, Wolf adopted him." With that, he looks at the others, "Its time people, time to go and do what we do best."

Ten minutes later we are in one of those white rooms that you always imagine scientists to work in. There is nothing in the room except the team and the Colonel. In front of us is the machine they call the 'Transputer'. It is bell-shaped; it has a heavy door with a glass window. Inside is a chair. Around the bell are a myriad of cables, lights and buttons, it is a work of art and even if it did nothing other than make a cappuccino, it would be an impressive piece of hardware. But this machine does more, so much more than make a cup of coffee. It is probably the second greatest scientific development in the history of mankind. I had been fully briefed, I knew my job, I knew the risk and I am in first. First in, first out.

"Will it hurt?" I say to Cross.

"No." She says with a confidence that is betrayed by her eyes.

I drop my gown; you had to enter the machine naked. I could have been more discreet, but that word is not in my vocabulary. Despite themselves both women look and quickly look away, the Colonel has a broad smile across his face.

I step into the machine and sit down. They'd briefed me, but they had given me scant information about this phase of the mission. I am the guinea pig, I am the first human to be 'done', I am going to be a hero, but right now all I want to know is how much will it hurt. The machine starts to buzz quietly, I can hear an audible countdown, TEN, it was all very civilized, NINE, no huge power pulses, EIGHT no arcing sparks, SEVEN no shaking, SIX 'Shit' I thought it's like Wolf's story again, FIVE, come on get on with it, FOUR, this was like being at the top of a big dipper.

THREE.

TWO.

ONE and then suddenly …………..

The War

The five men: Eckner, Lazenby, Blenkinsopp, Kruger and the Professor had gone to inspect the creature.

As they entered the room all they could see, where the creature had been encased in ice, was the shattered remains of its tomb. Large irregular blocks of ice scattered across the floor.

The group paused for only a moment on seeing the turmoil and almost as one, with courageous solidarity the men moved into the room so that they could see where that devilish trail of blood lead. Each had their own motivation; Eckner thought only of the safety of the crewman that he had ordered to guard the demonic giant; for both Blenkinsopp and the professor, fear must take a second place to their thirst for knowledge. Lazenby had an almost destructive wish for challenge, an insatiable desire to face his fear, already his thoughts were turning to a fateful battle with the creature, his nemesis. Of the group only Kruger had real fear, or at least, he lacked any greater motivation that could mask it – though no doubt he wanted the Key of Solomon.

As the group stood in silence they noticed a gurgling noise. The group edged around the door and the intervening boxes. There in all its brutality stood the monster, front legs standing bent on its unfortunate victim, its stinger raised high in the air, the creature poised like a sprinter in blocks, leaning forward, away from the men. Like sleepwalkers the group just stared at the grisly feast that was before them. Men show their true worth only under stress, Lazenby acted first leaping back across the room at the discarded Lugar pistol of the dead crewman. Blenkinsopp, despite his bulk deftly leapt back and disappeared from the room, not in fear, but in courage, he was brave enough to summon the troops – his courage was unquestionable. Eckner, was the next and last to do anything meaningful, he picked up the nearest heavy object, which happened to be a chair and foolishly threw it at the creature. It was a noble strike, the chair burst into pieces and would have undoubtedly felled a man but this was no man. The creature spun with lightning speed, its large claws whipping round, striking Eckner in the shoulder and almost knocked him from the room. This attack was unintended by the creature and probably saved Eckner, for its next attack was deadly. One claw flew at the throat of the still completely motionless Professor, whilst the evil sting flung itself at the forehead of Kruger. Lazenby saw the danger and picking up the nearest heavy object at hand threw himself in the path of the sting. A loud thump resonated around the room. A moment later Lazenby found himself prostrate next to Kruger, Lazenby had inadvertently grabbed the Key of Solomon, which he was holding 20cm in front of Kruger's face. Protruding through the book by 19cm was the knife like blade of the devil's sting.

The two men looked at each other for the briefest of seconds, both men felt a myriad of emotion, fear, gratitude, hatred, disgust, even humour. In that split second, Lazenby saw the irony of saving a Nazi occultist; by destroying that which Kruger most desired. The devil whipped back its sting, the book still attached, as the two struck the floor heavily. Lazenby span round to see the decapitated body of the noble professor; a jet of blood flew up, like his soul returning to heaven, his body stood momentarily before collapsing. Lazenby realised that this was not a fight he was going to win; grabbing the scruff of Kruger's shirt he dragged him through the door, emptying the complete magazine of the Lugar into the oncoming monster. The two fell through the door, but would certainly have been lost if not for Eckner slamming the door before the creature reached them, he twisted the lock – the creature was confined at least for now.

They stood there panting for a moment, Kruger looked sheepishly at Lazenby.

"Thank you, you saved my life."

Lazenby grinned back.

"Well nobody's perfect", then to Eckner, "can it get out?"

"The walls are thin wood, but inside the wall is the ships superstructure, the creature is strong but I doubt it could cut through, the only hole big enough is the floor hatch that we winched it up, whatever this creature is, it is contained, unless it can fly!"

"Did you....? Did you see what it....?" Kruger could not finish his words, he was suffering from shock. Lazenby heard before he saw, the troopers, their heavily shod boots rang out on the metal floor, as they came into view in the dimly lit service corridor. They darted down the corridor; men looking for a war, at the lead was Schumann, his tall frame not quite masking Blenkinsopp's portly shape.

"Two down – definitely dead." Lazenby spoke revealing his military background, a leader who had lost men before. Blenkinsopp popped around from behind Schumann.

"The Professor?" He said shaking his head. He was perspiring freely; a genius but no athlete. Schumann's men had now all arrived, he cocked his weapon, followed by almost a drum roll as his team cocked their weapons, following his unordered order. Schumann with a nod and collection of silent hand signals had his men posted and ready in seconds. Lazenby respected their professionalism and thought that if the Third Reich had many more men like this, then the war to follow the Great War would be a short one.

"Sir, you are injured," Schumann pointed to Eckner's shoulder, it had been sliced by the scorpion claw.

"I am not as bad as the man I ordered to his death!"

"Even so sir, you should get it looked at."

Then Lazenby, thinking ahead, asked Schumann for his knife. Schumann nodded to one of his men who handed over a vicious looking weapon.

"Let's see what our friend is doing, shall we?" With that, Lazenby forced the knife between the metal frame of the ship and the wooden divider. After a short moment's work he had prized a section of wood away. Lazenby then cautiously gazed in at the room beyond.

"What's it doing?" Blenkinsopp asked, still panting.

"It seems to be eating the crew member, no it has stopped, it's moving into the centre of the room, it's lowering itself…. I think it has gone to sleep… No wait! Good God, Blenkinsopp take a look at this."

Blenkinsopp moved to the hole. A moment later his eyebrows rose.

"Fascinating," he mumbled.

The Demon

Over Northern Atlantic nearing Scotland on the Hindenburg, March 1937, Wednesday 23:00 hrs.

"Gentlemen, let's get started." Eckner's voice carried authority and immediately had everybody's attention. The group had assembled in the hangar room, opposite the store. Present were all those of the previous meeting, except for the poor professor.

"Schumann, your report"

Schumann came to attention.

"I have secured the door to the store room with additional supports. I have arranged eight watches with three men on the door. I have posted a guard on the service corridor to ensure no passengers under any circumstances come down here. Finally, I have set up a heavy machine gun post facing aft, it has one thousand rounds."

"Good, well done." Eckner turned to a map on the wall, he grimaced from the pain of his heavily bandaged shoulder. He traced his hand across the map as he explained:

"As Captain of the Hindenburg I have set a course back to Germany, though if we require we can divert to Britain. I have made up a bad weather story, the passengers and most of the crew do not like it but they believe it. What about you Blenkinsopp?"

"Well," though Blenkinsopp tried to hide his enthusiasm, spy he may be, but as a scientist, he realised that this was the greatest discovery of the century, a broad smile broke out all over his face,

"Well, it is fascinating; the creature seems to have fed and on completion seems to have dropped into a semi-catatonic state. I am sure it would be safe; to study the creature closely now. What is amazing to me is that the creature is surely metallic."

Eckner broke in, 'What' do you mean? This monster is man-made!"

"Man-made, good God, No! And I don't think that it is a monster, it's a machine."

Kruger was in no mood for this type of discussion.

"I thought you were a scientist! You're telling us that it's a machine, but that it's not manmade. If men didn't make it, who did? Look all I say is that it is a monster, it nearly killed me today; we should kill it now while we have the chance."

"That's the sort of clap-trap I would expect from you" retorted Blenkinsopp and the conversation descended into a free for all.

"Wait!" Lazenby took control. "Sun Tzu said 'Know your enemy', I put a full magazine into this creature's face, it did nothing. This might give us a chance to find its weakness."

Then looking at Blenkinsopp who was visibly unhappy with the way the conversation was going,

"What we need are options if it does come to it."

"I should also tell you about its torso," said Blenkinsopp.

"I cannot see clearly through the hole but I can see swirling liquid in the torso, one can only guess at what it is doing, but it is obviously associated with food, perhaps it is its digestive system. The other main question we have is if it is a machine, what is its purpose? Machines are built to fulfil a task, remember its radio signal, which seems to have lessened in power. Of course, if it is an animal, it will have only one purpose, like all life, to survive and reproduce. Either way, we should be quick, before it stops doing whatever it is doing now."

Eckner made the decision.

"If you are volunteering, Blenkinsopp and Lazenby you can get a closer look. Schumann, you and your men cover them. I would remind you all, we are only doing this to learn how to kill it, it if makes a move Schumann, blow it to kingdom come.

Ten minutes later, the troopers had removed the additional barricade, the doors had been opened, four men in the door, plus an additional one through the hole cut by Lazenby, each had automatic weapons pointed at the beast. Lazenby and Blenkinsopp, the Anglo/American expedition, slowly, empty handed moved towards the demonic machine, still with the Key of Solomon firmly spiked to its tail.

"Easy Blenkinsopp", warned Lazenby

Blenkinsopp moved quickly up to the prone creature.

"Don't worry, it cannot attack until it stands up, we are quite safe." He put his hands on the creature, "My God, it's warm!"

He tapped it gently with a screwdriver; an audible metallic tone rang around the room. He inspected the thing, like a car salesman looking for every scratch and dent on a valuable car.

"Look Lazenby, you did hurt it, it bleeds, er… leaks."

Blenkinsopp pointed at a spider-like, multifaceted eye which was shattered, no doubt after a hit from the Lugar's 9mm round. The face of the creature was marked by a clear liquid, probably the contents of the shattered eye. Lazenby nodded.

"Well, a good shot in the left eye and the creature may be blinded and look, see these marks from the rounds."

"Barely, this creature's skin must have the strength of tensile steel."

Blenkinsopp moved down to the torso, the whole area was a semi-transparent, shimmering swirl of colour, mainly red but shot with blue and yellow.

"Amazing," he said as he moved his face close to the kaleidoscope of colour. Lazenby was busy looking at the creature's other eye.

"Good God!" Blenkinsopp leapt back away from the creature.

"Something moved, it tried to get to me, it was black, maybe a baby scorpion."

As Blenkinsopp gasped for air after his sudden shock, Lazenby had already pointed his pistol at the creature's good eye; then the beast started to move, but not quickly. It slowly raised its front and lowered its torso down to the deck. The steady swirl of its torso pulsed to a maddeningly psychedelic rhythm, the whole demonic shape shook to the same rhythm.

"What the hell is happening Blenkinsopp?"

"I think it is giving birth"

Lazenby summoned two more guards; who stood near the rear of the beast.

"You two, whatever comes out there, get your guns on it."

The two nodded in grim determination. Then the beast with one final shudder of tremendous power, gushed the same colourful liquid from its rear. In the jet of liquid, not a small scorpion or even a brood but a human or at least a humanoid. The thing laid there, prostrate for a moment, the guards were too shocked to fire, this was too much even for these hardened battle veterans. One muttered to himself.

"God help us, it is Satan himself."

Devil it could be, for it was black as the night, its body was sleek and wet, not a hair, ear or genitals protruded from its form. Its most striking feature were the eyes, black as coal and the size of large eggs. It rolled onto its stomach and raised itself onto all fours; it shook twice, opened a mouth, then vomited a litre of the red liquid on the floor. At this final act, all the men took an involuntary step back. A moment later these large eyes turned and fixed first on Blenkinsopp, then Lazenby and then each guard, for each man it was as if Death itself had walked across their graves. Even the troopers, these modern day knights of the third Reich were shaken, one in the room developed a noticeable damp patch on his trousers. To his shame the devil also noticed this, looking directly at this groin, for the guard, his shame was short lived.

The Scorpion beast having completed the birth returned to the initial part of its life cycle: food. It again, span towards Lazenby and Blenkinsopp and crouched ready for battle, the aggressive action drew an equally aggressive response. First to fire was a trooper in the door, immediately followed by all weapons. To be stood up in this bedlam was to die. Lazenby fired one well-placed shot at the creature's last good eye, then dropped taking Blenkinsopp with him. Then half crawling, half crouching he made for the door dragging a shouting Blenkinsopp, who was repeatedly screaming:

"Stop Firing!"

The blinded creature launched after the two of them, slowed by the energy of the machines guns. It shrugged off the 100 rounds of lead storm thrown at it. Blenkinsopp and Lazenby were already out, one the troopers tried to turn and run. A horrified Eckner looked on from the corridor. Just as he thought the trooper had escaped he suddenly stopped, his head flopping to one side, he then leapt into the air and disappeared back into the room, his body smashing and cracking with the impact on the door frame before he was gone. The Scorpion had grabbed him snapping his spine like a twig. The creature then slammed into the doorway, which barely held the onrush, bending from the impact.

Meanwhile, the two guards inside had both thought it prudent to put several rounds into the humanoid demon. It was knocked back, screaming, then lay still. Now they had a problem with the scorpion blocking the exit the only obvious way out was through the floor, but the ship was high in the clouds. Quick thinking one decided to go through the thin wooden walls of the room and break into the adjoining corridor. He leapt over the prone body of the demon and ran to the wall, his friend following, quickly realising his plan.

"Stand back! We are going to shoot out the wall," one shouted.

A face at the small hole shouted the same warning to the others in the corridor.

"Ok, go ahead."

A quick glance at the Scorpion confirmed that it had stopped moving and was feeding on the latest dismembered guard. With a confident grin at each other, they let rip with the state of the art twentieth-century firepower, the automatic weapons quickly pulped the wooden wall. As each weapon reported their 'Dead man's click', the firing pin having closed on an empty chamber, a black arm looped around one trooper's throat. The guard instantly dropped his weapon and desperately tried to protect his throat, but too late. The steel like arm had closed into a vice strong grip. The arm had formed a 'V' shape around the guard's throat, the other arm pulled the first together, causing huge pressure on the carotid arteries, two seconds later the guard was unconscious.

Meanwhile the other guard depended too much on his high tech weapon, to an age old low-tech problem, the butt of his weapon could have saved his companion, but instead, he went for a reload. Veteran as he was, two seconds was one second too few. He mechanically did the drill: magazine off, open his pouch, grab his new magazine, guide it into the weapon, all done to perfection, but for naught. The Demon having already dealt with the first guard, availed himself of his dagger. As the second trooper went to cock his weapon the dagger pierced his jugular and went through his throat. His life departed quickly in a crimson waterfall. He stood for a moment eyes on his nemesis, he tried to utter a prayer but his windpipe was cut, only a faint gurgle came, then he died.

Moments later a guard re-appeared at the small hole, to check on the troopers' progress, he had not expected a resurrected demon to have killed them.

"Arggggh!" He screamed, more in anger than fear and quickly jumped back so he could bring his weapon to bear through the hole. The demon was quicker and was already moving towards the Scorpion. What followed was a ballet to percussion, as the weapon rang out its 'ratatat', the demon hopped and rolled, leapt and bounced, skilfully avoiding the deadly, though badly aimed, hail of death, until he reached the safety of the Scorpion.

Schumann, blind to the events inside came to his men's rescue, with his corporal he shouldered the pulped wall, it gave way easily, he fell, rolled and with a dexterity to match the demon's, finished standing with his weapon aimed. His fast mind read the situation;

"Get them out of here!" His corporal dragged the two seemingly lifeless bodies, out through the hole.

Now the Demon reappeared, strangely just walking towards Schumann. Simultaneously, the trooper at the hole and Schumann let go a hail of bullets. As each struck a strange red glow answered. At first, Schumann thought itwas blood, but the creature just came on, again the 'dead man's click' reported. The Demon stopped only one step short from Schumann, stooped and picked up the dead trooper's machine gun, cocked it, pointed at Schumann, but then pointed it in the air and whilst laughing fired the entire magazine into the air. It was a chillingly human laugh.

The Birth

Unknown location with Major Lance.

Where am I? It's dark. I am in water, but I can breathe. Oh Shit! I feel a sudden falling feeling as I slide onto the floor. Bright lights. My eyes hurt. Get up, get on my feet. I am chocking. I vomit. Calm – think. Yes, they told me it would be like this, take a moment, get on top of it.

"Roarrrrr"

I hear a loud piercing roar from my side. I look and see the mangled remains of the X10 to my side. Towering above it is a huge lizard creature. Its mouth is the size of a sofa. It sees me and strikes – I roll to my left – too late!

"Argh......."

* *

Where am I? It's dark. I am in water, but I can breathe. Wow! What was that? I felt a large impact at my left-hand side. What the hell's going on? Think; yes they told me it would be like this. Yes, I am breathing the liquid, should be fun when I get that out of my lungs. Oh, why are the lights fading? Another large impact, this time, harder. Shit! I don't think this was in the manual.

"Bang."

Oh shit the X10 is rolling. I roll for what seems like an hour, each impact is worse than the last, then with one huge bone-crushing crunch.

"Arggggh!"

I feel extreme pain in my right leg, I think it is broken. All the lights are out on the X10 now. It's getting difficult to breathe, the breathing unit must be knocked out. Fresh air outside and I am lying in the womb of a dead mother – suffocating. I lash out recklessly, I try to kick, punch, claw my way out of this coffin, but the walls are too close, I can't get any power behind the blows.

My lungs start to wrench, they pull the liquid in, but there is no oxygen. Fucking hell I am going to DIE. I can hear the blood in my head pumping desperately as if that is going to make any difference.

"Of all _ the __ battles ___ I have ____ fought _____ I finish _____ up _____ here _____ a still _____ born _____.........."

* *

Where am I? It's dark. I am in water, but I can breathe. Oh shit! I'm suddenly falling as I slip onto the floor. Bright lights. My eyes hurt. Get up on your feet, well my hands and knees. I am chocking. I vomit. Calm – think. Yes, they told me it would be like this. Take a moment, get on top of it. Ok.

I look up and scan my environment. There, behind me is the X10, to my left are two men, thank God – I have found civilization, Professor Cross was right! One is heavy and slow, the other is slim and looks agile. I hold his eyes for a moment – there is fear, but courage too. He holds some sort of antique weapon in his hand. To my front are two men in uniform, clearly soldiers, both hold larger weapons. Odd, one has just pissed himself, Oh Shit! I am wearing the combat suit, what must I look like to these poor bastards? No sudden movements, the longer we stay like this the calmer everything will be, then I can slowly take off my face mask and we will be one big happy family. But, suddenly the X10 lunges forward, something must be wrong with it, it should not attack like that.

BANG, BA, BA, BANG

I am knocked backwards screaming; as the weapons fire four times. The soldiers have both double tapped me. Luckily they took torso shots, the combat suit stopped any penetration but not the pain, that'll be at least four broken ribs and God knows what internal damage. I lie still for a moment, I do not want to attract any more fire. The two guards leap over me and fire at the wall, they are apparently trying to get out. They have their backs to me, it is payback time. I have only three things on my mind, first, get a weapon, second get my armour pack and then achieve my primary mission, to secure the area.

I roll over and stand up, it hurts like hell, for a moment the world fades, comes back, fades again, but I get control. It's not hard to move up behind the two guards, they are emptying their magazines into the wall. I had seen weapons like theirs in the museums. I suppose given the human form and basic physics, where ever in the universe I am now, the design of a weapon will be practically the same. But these are not energy weapons like I use, but instead work on controlled explosions. I know that they will have a limited number of shots; when I hear the click, I attack. I do not want to kill the soldiers so the first one I choke out, I wrap my arm around his neck in a scarf hold, pull him tight into my body, lift slightly and in seconds it's over. The other guy is trying to reload, no time for niceties, I take the first soldier's knife and ram it into the second's throat. Killing a man is never easy, killing a man like this is the worse, he stands for a moment his eyes look straight at me. I don't know whether they show fear, does he try to utter a prayer, maybe he's begging, either way, he tries to talk but his throat is gone. I'll never forget his eyes, it gets personal when you get this close; but I've done it before and, like then, I will get over it. I am not a cold-blooded killer, I am professional, but I dream like everybody else.

A face appears through a hole in the wall, he is shouting. I start to move, the barrel of a weapon is pushed through the hole. I start to swerve, roll and dive as the world around me explodes, as does the pain in my sides. I get to the back of the X10, I am safe, it is immune to these rounds. I sit for a moment, the symphony of explosions still rings about me, I am nauseous, a body can only take so much pain before your brain closes down. I am fighting a losing battle for consciousness, for a moment I waver on the edge, I teeter; but I have work to do and I am not done yet. I bite hard into my cheek, taste the blood, focus and get back on top of it. I turn around, open the tiny stores compartment on the X10 and pull out the shield unit, I also knock back a pain killer. I push the shield into place at my lower back. I learnt many years ago, when it gets down and dirty like this, the winners are the ones who want it the most and show it. It is time for some bravado. I stand, immune to their weapons, at least for a while, this will seriously deplete the power cells, but I have always thought, use what you have, when you have it.

The soldiers, who have reloaded by now, empty a magazine each at me, this time, they bounce off me harmlessly, God I love technology. I am about to pass out with pain, but first I must define my domination. I reach down and pick up the soldier's weapon, cock it, point it at the roof and empty the magazine whilst laughing, long, loud and hard. It has the required effect, in moments I am alone, they are brave, they don't run, they withdraw. I step behind the X10, which is feeding, slide down its body until I hit the deck.

"Time to pass out," I say and I do.

The Plan

Over the North Atlantic on the Hindenburg, March 1937, Thursday 1:00 hrs.

Eckner had assembled the group. Everyone was in the officers' mess.

"We all agreed for various reasons to bring that thing on my ship and now five people have died. I want ideas for how we are going to progress, but these things are clear, first, I must protect the passengers, next the ship and then third, of course, the crew. If I can I will return the ship to Germany, I have already talked to my officers and we have devised a way that we can get the passengers off, in these extreme circumstances; I fear any moment that creature will come forward and start wholesale slaughter." He paused for a moment, the gruesome deaths of his crew were clearly etched on his face. "What I want from you is to assess, how we deal with these creatures, their strengths, weaknesses and motivation, Schumann what is your report?"

"As you know I have lost two of my men, though we managed to recover the body of one, the other was choked unconscious and has now recovered."

Blenkinsopp interrupted,

"But you said five had died if your man recovered? I only make four."

Lazenby tried to show no expression on his face, Blenkinsopp still did not know about Mörder.

An embarrassed Eckner spoke up.

"Oh, yes, four, even so, you're right it is four, but it matters not, we still need a plan, continue Schumann."

"I have fully debriefed him, he says he and Köln both fired at the demon and it definitely went down and screamed, though he recollects that it did not bleed. It then got up and came behind him and put a choke hold on him. He says it had a grip like steel and it took him out very quickly, he can't remember anything else. It seems that it then knifed Köln in the throat. Hengst then opened fire and it dodged all the rounds, though Hengst had only a limited view of the room so his fire was not too accurate. By that time I had gone through the wall and got my men out, it reappeared from behind the Scorpion and both Hengst and I emptied our magazines at it, each round just bounced off it and it laughed at us. Later it came into the corridor but dodged the rounds from the MG34 heavy machine gun."

Eckner looked next at Lazenby.

"The Scorpion seems to be contained, I managed to put another round into its other eye, though it must still have some sensors, as it grabbed one of Schumann's men. It tried to come through the door, but was stopped, I do not think it can get through any hole, bar the trap door; though I fear what would happen if it made a really concerted effort."

"As for the demon, it is a conundrum. It can be downed by bullets, unless it was a ruse, but why bother if it was immune? It attacks a man, extremely efficiently, it is no coincidence that it used a sleeper hold, how would an alien know that? It then dodges bullets to return to the Scorpion but then stands idly to be shot at, whilst laughing and firing in the air when it could have killed you Schumann, why? Finally, it again dodges bullets of the MG34 machine gun. Is it bulletproof, does it draw power from the Scorpion, is it getting more powerful, why does it not come and kill everybody now?"

"Mr. Blenkinsopp," asked Eckner, "can you cast some light on the problem?"

"As Lazenby says, it's a conundrum but what is most interesting is what it has not done, why did it not kill one trooper, but did the other?"

Schumann jumped in, unskilfully showing too much emotion and his opinion.

"It fought as best it could, it would definitely have killed him if it had the chance."

"Then why did it not kill you Schumann? I don't think so. It was shot at and retaliated with a non-lethal response, it then killed when it was given no choice.

Lazenby was shaking his head,

"But what about the scorpion, it has attacked and murdered three men in cold blood."

"I don't believe that the Scorpion has intelligence, not like the man." It was the first time anybody had referred to the Demon as a man. "I think the Scorpion is just like an insect, it works like an insect, if it is hungry it gets food and it eats. That food sadly happens to be a sentient life force."

"I am not buying it," said Schumann, "the Demon laughed at us when we shot at it, the damned thing is playing with us."

"My point exactly," said the excited Blenkinsopp, "The creature demonstrated its supremacy without harming you, it is like when a child hits you – you laugh."

Lazenby too was unconvinced, "I think it is more complex than that, I do not think this thing is invincible; it has a weakness, one that it is trying to cover up, we need to test it, to see what its weakness really is."

Blenkinsopp stood up in agitation,

"Look, the Professor would agree with me if he were here, God rest his soul."

Eckner spoke,

"Yes, but he is not here, he has been murdered by those creatures and I also remember him saying they were alien and dangerous. The agenda here gentlemen is how do we kill these things, it's that simple!"

"But give me a chance to talk to them, it's my decision, it's my risk."

Eckner was adamant that no more should die, he shook his head repeatedly,

"I am the captain of this ship, whilst on board, you are my responsibility, I will not allow you to take such a foolhardy risk."

"So be it" Blenkinsopp accepted the command, but not only was he a brilliant engineer, he was also a brilliant spy, he was already hatching his plans. Meanwhile, Lazenby was doing what he did best.

"The only way to be sure would be to get everybody off the ship and blow the whole thing to kingdom come."

"We have explosives and fuses with us," offered Schumann.

"Nobody is going to blow up the Hindenburg," said Eckner staring at them angrily. But Lazenby and Schumann were soldiers, they were both thinking about the bigger picture. One professional nodded to the other, unnoticed by the others, there would be a bomb – as the final solution.

"Should we try rushing them?" It was the first thing Kruger had said. Each man looked around the room if not that what else would they do?

"Sheer firepower might overwhelm them." said Schumann very unconvincingly.

"The scorpion has been wounded, though whether we can kill it – I don't know," said the equally unconvinced Lazenby.

"A sticky bomb might do it." added Schumann.

"On an airship. Think again." said Eckner.

"It would seem", said Blenkinsopp with a shrug, "that all our really effective weaponry will blow us all to kingdom come. I suggest we prepare our defences, try to get the passengers off, then fly to Germany, where we can come within Heliograph range and prepare an appropriate reception. In the meantime, we should do nothing proactive."

That seemed to pretty well sum up everybody's thoughts, so it was agreed. Eckner went over his plans for off-loading the passengers, a difficult and dangerous task with no landing stations, no winch, no radio and an imminent potential massacre if the demon got loose.

Finally, he asked:

"Lazenby and Blenkinsopp, you are neither crew nor German officers, would you wish to be disembarked with the passengers?"

Kruger was of one mind,

"They have no right or role aboard, they should be landed."

Blenkinsopp smiled his best smile, "Captain Eckner, this is much bigger than nation, this could be of world importance, Lazenby and I have been closer to these things than anyone here, our knowledge may be invaluable. I am now the only scholar on board and Lazenby is the only one to injure it, I implore you, let us stay."

Eckner disliked Kruger intensely and all that he stood for, he looked to another man in a German uniform for support, Schumann nodded,

"It is decided, you will stay and we thank you for your courage. One final thing, the gunfire has punctured at least one gas bag, I am sending a team up to try and repair it. It could cause us a problem if we continue to lose Hydrogen, we would probably not make Germany. But if we disembark the passengers the ship should have enough lift, but please do not fire any weapons, except in the direst of circumstances."

"You can get men on top of the ship whilst it is flying?" asked the quick thinking Lazenby.

"Why Yes."

"Is there an inspection shaft behind, sorry, aft of the store room?" Eckner nodded.

"Yes," said Schumann realising where Lazenby was going with this, "Then perhaps we should take a look down there, it would be useful to get behind them, we could then communicate via the aft steering room."

Eckner was shaking his head,

"It is too risky, we are moving into a storm, we do not have the time to go around, I would only send experienced crew into such conditions."

Lazenby was not to be denied,

"Desperate situations require desperate measures, let's get moving gentlemen, I am going for a promenade on the top of the world." He winked at Blenkinsopp, span round and left the room, effectively ending the meeting.

The Ditching

Orkneys, Scapa Flow, March 1937, Thursday 04:00 hrs. On Admiral Fisher's flagship HMS Hood.

"Sir five miles and closing" reported a young lieutenant.

"What the hell is going on Sir? This time the Captain of the Hood. A commander of a ship has always been a position of responsibility, a position held only by the most capable and courageous men and none more so than in the Royal Navy. Such an admission of was a rare thing indeed, but it was an admission that even Admiral Fisher must also make and he a man that held the same command as the legendary Nelson held at Trafalgar. The Royal Navy had also been monitoring the signal from the North Pole, as had, the Admiral was sure, every nation in the northern hemisphere. He had sent ships from Canada and Scapa Flow, but none could match the speed of the Hindenburg and the British R101 airship was currently being refitted. Even so, they had monitored the Hindenburg and had followed her on her return trip, not difficult with such a powerful signal, though it had weakened noticeably to only half the original strength. A fact that had directly caused the panic, when the latest triangulation placed the ship not 100 miles but only 50. It had kept closing. The Admiral wondered what the hell they were doing.

In normal times nobody was allowed to fly over Scapa Flow and in these troubled days it would verge on an act of war. He would wait and see what would occur, one thing he felt sure of, the Hindenburg was a passenger ship with no military capability.

"The fighters should be alongside by now Sir, funny we have not had a signal yet."

"Try and raise them again," said the Captain to the communications officer.

"What does Cromwell report?" asked the Admiral referring to a destroyer sent out to get a visual of the Hindenburg.

"We have no message from her either."

The Admiral turned and gave the Comms. Officer a withering look,

"My god man, sometimes no message is as crucial as 'A' message; tell me who has a visual of the Hindenburg and has reported it"

"Er.., well, no one Sir."

"There are 50 ships between us and the Hindenburg, someone has to be able to see her and tell us"

"Yes, Sir, er.. I mean No Sir."

The Captain looked at the Admiral and he looked back, then as if they were in the middle of a hand of bridge with the vicar and his wife, in total calm the admiral said

"We will have battle stations", he turned to the Comms. Officer, "Battle stations for the fleet and I want a list of who replies."

The ship burst in action, the Captain and Admiral stood like lighthouses in a storm of activity. Admiral Fisher looked at the ships at anchor through his binoculars, he checked the sky where the Hindenburg would soon be, Starboard 20'. Then looked back to his fleet; odd nothing was happening, he thought. Then the whistle of the voice pipe.

"Bridge" answered the XO (executive officer). He put the piece to his ear, then reported.

"Admiral, we have lost radar."

Then, as white as a ghost, the Comms. Officer, "Sir, no ships are responding, I think we have lost comms."

Then the XO, "Cleared for Battle stations," he announced to no one in particular. The Captain turned to his Comms. Officer,

"Don't THINK, KNOW man! You know the Royal Navy used to work quite adequately without radio!" He nodded to the XO, moments later flashes were seen rebounding across the fleet, the

Morse code of the lamps, closely followed by "Whoop, Whoop" of 50 Royal Navy ships replying to the flagship's siren.

"Captain, I see a light Green 20"

"Green 20, Aye" repeated the captain as twenty binoculars swung to that bearing.

"Let's light her up captain" ordered the Admiral. The ship's huge search lights were quickly brought to bear onto the Hindenburg, not enough power from this distance, but every other ship in the fleet and the shore bases followed suit, in 30 seconds Scapa Flow was an intricate crisscross of light.

"It must be like a summer's day on board the Hindenburg," quipped an able seaman, who had no place talking on the bridge, but, it helped to relieve the tension.

Soon the bulk of the Hindenburg came into full view. Even Admiral Fisher was impressed by it grace and size, a thing floating in the air, which in size match the Hood herself.

"She is descending Sir, about 300 foot"

"Looks like she is going to land, well ditch, she must be in trouble Admiral."

"Yes, let's have the boats away"

"Sir, the gunners man the boats!"

"Yes, stand down the big guns and do the same on Rodney and Somerset"

Three minutes later and a small flotilla of boats was heading for the Hindenburg. Scapa Flow is a natural harbour made by a circle of islands, the water had only a small swell. Admiral Fisher watched as the ship came down to just above the water and hovered.

The comms. Officer came into the bridge and handed the admiral a message. The Admiral smiled wryly,

"Do they think that we will swallow that," then reading out loud, "PLAGUE ON BOARD STOP ISOLATED ON SHIP STOP WILL DROP PASSENGERS FOR SAFETY STOP."

Almost on cue, small splashes were seen as the passengers abandoned ship, each quickly picked up by one of the many small boats.

Admiral Fisher observed,

"Whatever the truth, it's a bad day for Germany when they have to throw their passengers in front of British warships!"

The Briefing

Over Scotland on the Hindenburg, March 1937, Thursday 06:00 Hrs.

I come to with a start, it takes only a split second to remember the key word – DANGER. My body immediately goes into overdrive, I roll over and stand up crouching, automatically checking the safety is off of my weapon. I had passed out many times in action for one reason or another and my almost inhuman sense of self-preservation had saved my life at least once. But not this time. I stand there for only one heartbeat before my body erupts in the pain of moving with broken ribs.

"Fuck, that hurts." I mutter quietly to myself. It all comes rushing back to me, the birth, the battle and me passing out behind the X10. I slowly stand up fully, I am pretty sure I am alone, but it is good to check. My stomach wrenches with the pain, I would have thrown up if I had eaten anything in the last 27 years. I am alone and I slide down the X10 and pop another pain killer. My attention is caught by the weapon which is lying across my knees. Here I am half way across the universe and something as simple as safety catch works exactly the same here as it does at home – it's a small world, well universe. I rest for a moment and wait for the drugs to kick in, I think of home, I think about the mission briefing. It seemed so easy then. Dr. Moon was a feisty old lady; I liked her, though I don't think the feeling was mutual. Lazlo was the type of guy you could depend on. I look forward to his arrival, loneliness is hard, but on an alien planet, it would soon become unbearable. The Professor was also a capable woman, apparently she was on the team for two reasons, to ensure the team ran smoothly and to integrate with any intelligent life we encountered. Personally, I was in charge of security, Lazlo was in charge of the well-being of the party, food, shelter and the like. The Colonel had given us the overview briefing.

"You have all had the chance to meet now. Some of you have been involved in this from the beginning, others, like you Lance have just come on board. This briefing is to ensure everybody understands the mission objectives, issues and equipment. Some of you have already been training with the equipment, well bits of equipment. I will explain this in due course, first the mission." He paused for effect.

"Our planet's resources are slowly being used up. So far, our scientist, have solved each shortage and found alternatives. Clearly, where we need to be is in the stars, finding new planets to colonise. The problem, as every schoolboy knows, is that we are limited in range, we have colonised one planet and a couple of moons, but even the nearest solar system will take thousands of years to reach. But, we have a secret weapon, Dr. Moon" He nodded at our leader. "She is the physicist who has been working on folding space. In essence take a map if you wish to travel from point A to point B you fold the map so the points touch, you then step from one to the other. This technology is known in fantasy and science fiction as 'Gates'. Dr. Moon has made it a reality. I hope Doctor that I explained that correctly?"

"Yes, thank you Colonel."

"Would you explain the challenge please, Doctor."

The elegant Dr. Moon stood and flashed her smile, she looked like a child opening a present.

"I first proved this theory only three years ago, when I published a well-received paper, it barely made the news, though our government thought it sufficiently important to support. Last year we set up a gate between the moon 'Scythus' and here, it is still top secret, but soon we will connect the entire solar system.

The team despite themselves looked at this little old lady with a new admiration.

"The problem is you can only 'jump' to a gate, which means you have to get somewhere, build a gate and then jump freely to and fro. A gate, therefore, is not a tool to explore a new world, it is a tool to colonise it. However, by chance I read a summary of an article of a new development in genetics, it is a machine called a weaver. It can literally weave DNA into anything – like a new hand for Lazlo, it effectively clones items but these machines were incredibly expensive and for moral reasons could never be used on whole humans. Really, the whole thing, whilst phenomenal technology was a white elephant; it was a solution looking for a problem. It got me thinking though, what if we could deliver a Weaver unit across the universe that could produce clones to build a gate. That was one year ago – the last piece of the jigsaw falls into place in two days. How I wondered could I get these clones around the universe – a Vortex I thought." Again she paused, this was like watching a movie, the team was mesmerised.

"A Vortex is a very rare astronomical event, it is like a whirlpool in space, a natural gate, it happens rarely and even rarer is a predictable Vortex. There has only been two in recorded history, or at least in the last 3000 years that we could predict. They have often been thought of as a means of travelling through space but they throw you out anywhere and can also distort time. We thought that if we could throw enough cloning devices into the Vortex, some would seed on planets. We have fitted a special device to maximise the chance of hitting a planet. For the last year an effort never seen in peacetime, thousands of scientists and engineers have been working towards a deadline – a one in 1500 year window. For a year we have been getting ready production lines for the output and shipment of the weavers, we have nearly one million units sitting in space."

"Wow, that is a big number" Lazlo was rapidly reaching overload.

"Yes it's a big number, it represents the equivalent of a small country's total annual manufacture capability."

"If I may now continue Doctor?" Asked the Colonel, she nodded politely and sat down.

"You can envisage an operation like this has taken time to get together, some parts were easier, others harder, so the personnel, hardware and software have not been complete until today."

He looked at each straight in the eyes as he explained the mission.

"Your mission is to go through the Transputer, which will code you and your memory, this data will be uploaded to the Weaver units, which in turn will be inserted into the Vortex. You, by tomorrow, will be safe and tucked up at home, I told you it was any easy mission, Lance!" He beamed at me, it broke the tension a little.

"For your clones, however, which will think they are you; they will face a very difficult task of building a gate on a foreign and perhaps very alien planet."

"A word about the equipment, the military have provided the X10, this is a six-limbed walker, designed for insertion and reconnaissance and as a weapon's platform. It is the upgrade to the X9 which you are already familiar with Lance. Lazlo has also studied it. The Weaver has been mounted on the X10, with a feeding mechanism, the Weaver needs to process materials to build the DNA. There is an extremely small storage facility for energy cells and other required kit. Remember the Weaver can process any biological materials, food, drugs, even a few plants."

"So", I said, "Maybe on an alien planet but I can still have a steak and a beer."

Nobody laughed, though I thought it was funny.

"We have developed," the Colonel continued, "a special body armour made from spider web which will actually be grown onto you, though you can take if off. You have a full face mask and developed from a special lightweight chitin material, like a beetle's shell, to give the armour more protection. The suit material is like difficult to puncture, but will offer only a little protection from a blunt trauma. Lance, you also have one P20 body shield. Again space is at a premium, we have embedded in your clones a small computer which will sit behind your brain. It will give each of you specialist knowledge and language abilities. We have picked for each of you a library of medicine, physics, engineering so, even you Lance should be capable of building a gate. The language unit is really an enhanced memory tool if you understand a foreign word it will automatically log its language and meaning. In tests, users have mastered a language in less than four hours, though this assumes you are being taught."

"The most important piece of kit is the Gate core. This complex technology is the heart and brain of the Gate, you will need advanced technology to build another one, so without it – mission over. It is mounted in the X10. Oh, and Professor Cross has something she'd like to add."

"Yes, thank you Colonel, I think this might cheer us all up a little before we finish. As you know I specialise in genetics, but inevitably studying this field and particularly in the context of what we are doing I have for some time focussed on Xenology, or the study of aliens. Although, as you will hear, that phrase might not be appropriate, so if you bear with me a moment I'll explain my views. OK, where should I begin? Right, I've got it. We are about to enable our race to travel to the stars and in this, we will be successful. Now if you have an almost infinite number of stars and an infinite amount of time, I think it is safe to say that this has happened before and will happen again. Are you with me so far Major Lance?"

I nodded, I was with her, but I had no idea where we were going.

"So we have established that there have already been space travellers, OK? Now, with my work in biology and genetics I can tell you that in our long, long history on this planet our DNA has not changed, at all, ever." She paused expecting us to have some sort of epiphany, it didn't happen.

"Well, what I am saying is that in the 100,000 years of our history, we have not evolved, because evolution takes a very, very long time. Yes, nature can cook up some basic bugs, even worms and the like, but not bees that can fly, not warm blooded creatures, not something as complex as a brain. Take the eye, take one element away and it stops working. How do you evolve a lens, an eyelid, a cornea, the senses, the brain, all at once? You don't, at least not often enough, not often enough for us to be here on this planet, unless of course, we happen to be the one total exception in the universe. What I am saying is if advanced life is a statistical anomaly and if space travel is possible, then we are in fact all Aliens.

Again she waited for it to sink in.

"Are you still with me Wolf?"

"Er, can you repeat everything after, Thank you Colonel." He grinned like a hyena. He was like me, we were both thinking, 'So what?'

Moon understood the problem,

"What the Professor is saying is that evolution like ours is so rare, it is more likely that we have come from another planet than evolved on this one. It, therefore, follows that if humans have colonised an alien planet, then they will have colonised many planets." As she was finishing her sentence she was slowly nodding like a primary school teacher. Me and Wolf were nodding back at her, the penny was starting to drop.

"So", I said, "I really might be able to have a steak and a beer."

Still nobody laughed.

With that, the first briefing was over. Strange it all seems like yesterday, to me it is, but when I checked the X10's chronometer it was 27 years ago. Strange that at home I would now be an old man, I may even be dead. In some ways I will probably never die, there are one million Lances who will just keep popping up, maybe forever. But right now I don't have time for such thoughts, to me here and now I have one life – I intend to live it!

The painkiller is starting to work so I get to work, first I survey the area, my primary mission was to protect the team. I strip the dead bodies of their kit; I find several quite complex weapons, my complete haul is two pistols, one long gun which only seems to hold about ten rounds and the weapon that I had already fired that holds a long magazine with about 30 rounds. This last gun seems the most effective, particularly for close quarters, so I keep it, there are also three daggers. I have about 200 rounds in total, but surprisingly they are of three different types. I try to assess the situation as best I can, but I cannot recce. the place properly. My role is to stay here and protect the team, I would have to wait for Lazlo, that is his job. Even so with a weapon store and my own personal gun, I decide to at least check the immediate vicinity.

First, I check the door, it is pretty messy, the X10 had literally ripped a man apart by pulling him through it and the X10 is still busy assimilating the body; or at least that is the term the scientists used for this ghoulish act of cannibalism. I check the X10 it looks pretty beat up, it must have been damaged, there is no way it should have attacked humans, even alien humans if you know what I mean. What is odd, there seems to be an old book stuck to its antennae. I then carefully look past the X10. I can see a room opposite across a narrow corridor, the floor of which is made of a metal grid. I can hear guards up the corridor to my left. On taking a quick look I can see they have a heavy weapon, I doubt my shield can take many hits from that. As I duck my head back in, I hear rounds fly down the corridor, their intentions are clear, as are the speed of their reactions. The wall adjoining the corridor is pretty well wrecked, where the soldiers had first shot and then kicked through, in addition, there is a small hole in the wall between here and the door. There are some heavy boxes in the room that looked like they contained mechanical parts, I push these forward to block both holes.

At first, I had assumed I was in a building, there was a droning noise, so I thought it was either a factory or perhaps underground and that it might be air conditioning units. However, looking at the wall opposite to the corridor I have the disturbing view of the ground, a long way down. I found a trap door with a winch, which was probably how the X10 had been loaded into the ship, for ship it must be, though I have no idea how it is moving so slowly in the air, especially with this world's low technology. I can see Lazlo was about to 'pop out of the oven', but I have enough time to look at the aliens, after a couple of minutes I am sure they are human like me – I would leave it to Professor Cross to explain that one.

With an unpleasant slurping followed by a gushing noise, Lazlo slips out of the X10's womb. He does the same as me, looks stunned, rolls over, for some reason painfully smashing his hand into the floor, he vomits the embryonic fluid and says for his first ever word:

"SHIT!"

Looking at him I realise what a shock my birth must have been to the dead guards – it is pretty disgusting, a human sized 'fly thing' popping out of a scorpion monster – wow!

Lazlo is sitting up, stroking his hand, then I realise; it is his missing hand, when he had rolled over his brain tried to put a stump on the floor. He looks at me, grinning and holds it up:

"A whole new world of wanking."

I reach out and pull him up by his new hand, we hug, it is a good moment. No matter how much time I have spent alone behind enemy lines, you never get used to it, I now have a comrade, he too is happy to see a friendly face (well under a combat suit). He has come to a friendly world, or so he thinks at this point. I quickly brief him on the situation and we discuss our next step. Lazlo decides to check over the X10,

"It's running blind, both sensory panels are down, from what you say its brain must be a little frazzled, it should never have attacked intelligent creature's, particularly humans. I'll get the diagnostics running if we want the rest of the team we need food."

"Well, we are in a store room, must be something in here."

Sure enough within five minutes we find several boxes of small metal containers with meat and others with vegetables. We even find several crates of bottles, which I assume are some sort of alcoholic beverage.

"There are definite advantages of finding a planet with humans!" I beam at Lazlo. We set away the X10 unit processing the food, with a small stash set aside for the team.

"Lazlo, you are going to have to get the lie of the land."

"Is there any way out? I think the corridor sounds too dangerous." He asks

"We can go out the corridor, trap door or one of the walls."

Lazlo goes to the wall of the ship.

"It looks like cloth." He picks up one of the daggers and slashes a large hole and pops his head through, a moment later he is gone.

The Gamble

"Excuse me," Blenkinsopp smiled as he squeezed by the machine gun post, some 20 paces aft of the store room.

"Sir, the lieutenant said no one was allowed past here."

It was too late, he was already waddling down the corridor.

"Don't worry son, I am an American citizen, what your Lieutenant says, has nothing to do with me."

Schumann appeared behind his troopers.

"Blenkinsopp, don't be mad you will be killed."

Blenkinsopp turned.

"You see that is the trouble with you Europeans, a millennium of war, you don't trust anybody, I come from a country where different nationalities trust each other", he winked and turned away again,

"See you in hell gentlemen."

Schumann said to no one in particular "Fools and Angels."

A trooper said prophetically to the other,

"One day America will stop trusting!"

As Blenkinsopp walked down the corridor, he had his hands in the air. He had a momentary image of the gunfight of the OK Corral with the Erp brothers wearing head holsters, hands poised high over their heads. He hoped that the alien would understand such a gesture if they wore weapons on their heads he was in trouble. He wanted to avoid the scorpion, it was mindless and could just kill him, he felt confident though that the demon was intelligent and that no intelligent life would kill another out of hand. Blenkinsopp was the eternal optimist, even his most recent foray into spying had not dented this, why and even how he

118

could separate a murderous demon from his own murderous brethren seemed bizarre. Why would he think intelligent life could not be sadistic, cruel and murderous, had he forgotten man's history? He was whistling loudly, he did not want to surprise anyone. He planned to enter at the ruined wall but it was blocked, this was unfortunate he did not wish to put his head through a hole in the wall, nor did he want to face the scorpion. He had no choice, he slowly edged around the door, the scorpion was back in its gestation period. That was a relief though short lived. The alien rose up from behind the scorpion, a sub machine gun levelled directly at him. Well he thought to himself,

"He has not fired, that must be a good sign," he was after all always the optimist.

* *

I hear voices again, but, with no reference, the language computer can make nothing of it. Someone is walking down the corridor, I can hear whistling. I move behind cover, they may use grenades. I can only hear one man, the talking has finished, he pauses behind the hole. I level the weapon below the hole if anything comes through the hole I will take the percentage shot, low and left; the full magazine. No, he moves past the hole, he is coming round the door. He is clearly afraid of the X10- he has his hands up, looks like a parley – good.

I beckon him in, he smiles and steps forward, he steps carefully around the X10. It could be a trap, I back up to the crates, so no one can see me through the hole. I motion for him to sit, he kneels, still with his arms in the air. I put one hand on my head, he understands and puts both hands on his head.

He is old and fat, not a warrior, he is dressed differently to all those with weapons.

I circle behind and search him. He has a handful of metal discs, some paper and what I think is an antique writing device. I go back to my safe position, as an act of good will, I put my weapon across my knees. He smiles again. God, I wish Professor

Cross was here, this is her job. The man looks up at me and as plain as day says:

"Hello"

It shook me for a moment until I realise it must be the computer.

"Hello," I say back.

He starts to laugh.

Minutes later we are playing charades, it is like a kid's party. He is an intelligent man and lays down a textbook like summary of his language, each time I repeat the word, he runs, walks, swims, looks, speaks, sits stands, each time pronouncing the word. At first, he tests me, but he soon realises that I never forget a word. After 10 minutes I realise that I am in full-face armour, I slip my hood off, he is overjoyed.

"Human", He announces proudly, "Me Blenkinsopp"

"Yes, Human", I reply, "Me..."

I pull out my dagger and put in on the end of a pole.

"Lance", he says, "Hello, Lance and welcome."

He looks around and sees a packing crate, a moment later and he is standing holding two bottles.

"Beer, Becks Beer."

I am really starting to like this guy.

He pops the tops off the bottles hands me one.

He clatters his bottle against mine and immediately the drink froths over the bottle top, I think I know what this beer stuff is.

"Lance, a toast – Long Life!"

"Long Life." I reply and gulp down half the bottle and yes this 'beer' is exactly what I thought it was, all I needed was a steak.

For the next 20 minutes, all was forgotten, we revel in language, for me it is amazing – I have never been good with languages and to learn this language, which is apparently called 'German' is wonderful. Once I had a pretty good mastery of the language, it was time to turn to business. Lazlo was still on reconnaissance and would soon return.

"What this?" I say gesturing at the ship.

"It is Hindenburg, it lighter than air."

"What….?" I move my hand in the air and pointed up to it.

"Ah, what keep it in air?" The language computer was wonderful, every time he said something that I understood – it was there to use at will, though it would take a long time to get the grammar sorted out.

He laughs and then stood thinking, he is evidently working out how to explain something quite complex to me. He grabs a handful of air.

"Air"

"Yes, Air, we breathe it." I reply.

He then draws a line on the floor and divides it into three-quarters, to the larger side he points.

"Nitrogen", to the smaller, "Oxygen."

I nod, I understand.

"Oxygen burns" I add.

He then says,

"Water", we had learnt this one earlier, "One part Hydrogen, two parts Oxygen."

I nod, again happy that I understand,

"Hydrogen, it is lighter than air." I say.

He points up, my smile dropped off my face, I make a noise of an explosion, shaking my head in disbelief.

"Yes," he says, "Big bomb!"

These crazy people are floating around under a huge bag of hydrogen and firing weapons, maybe they were not as civilized as I had thought.

I then hear shouting and running. I pick up my weapon and slip my mask back on. Blenkinsopp leaps up,

"I stop them!"

He bursts into the corridor waving his arms over his head.

"No, No, No!" he screams.

That's when I make my first mistake, I follow. I don't know why, whether it was instinct, perhaps I wanted to help my new ally, maybe an even friend, either way, it was a bad mistake.

The Safe Birth

"Welcome back," says the Colonel.

"How long have I been out?" I say, still with a very unpleasant taste in my mouth.

"72 hours, your genes are out populating the universe, here is a towel, there's a gown on the chair."

I notice there are lots of white-smocked scientists milling around in the background. I towel off the slime from my body – it stinks, badly.

"I thought you said I would have armour on?"

"Yes, you would." It is a women's voice. I turn round to be confronted by a stunningly attractive woman, dark hair, almond eyes, probably early twenties.

"But", she continues, "You are not getting into a dangerous environment here, so we left it out."

"If I knew science was this interesting I might have stuck in with the maths. How does an old soldier get a date with you?"

She smiles, cruelly.

"Well I've two good bits of news for you: first, you are no longer old and secondly you have just signed up for one million dates with me, so sooner or later you will score – after all a few of my clones are bound to be brain damaged – I am Doctor Moon."

I am not often lost for words, but this is one of the occasions, my brain simultaneously trying to compile this beautiful woman, the clones and the fact that one million 'mes' will be with one million 'hers' and as an afterthought the fact that she has just totally blown me away. After much too long a time to qualify as a comeback:

"Well aren't you a lucky women to have a million dates with me!" It is not fast, it is not clever, nor is it particularly me, I regret it as soon as I say it – I regret it more a moment later.

"Well, Soldier," she mimics a macho stance, "We are both lucky, You because we've cured your piles and Me because we've also removed your three venereal diseases."

There is a peal of laughter from around the room, the Colonel covers his mouth with his hand but his shoulders shake, at least he tries not to rub it in.

"I surrender", I say smiling, let's start again, "Lance, Professional asshole, I'm sorry."

She shakes my hand enthusiastically, "Maybe you're not the complete jerk I thought you would be." Her smile is quite wicked, she is obviously enjoying the attention her new body is getting her. I am tempted to ask her how long it has been since she has had sex but I have lost two rounds, I do not fancy going for three. It then occurs to me if she looks like that, what the hell do I look like? A quick look at my body reveals a physique that I always imagined I had, but could never quite get, all my scars have gone, I feel great. I am once again in the flower of my manhood. Another scientist hands me a mirror, I have hair! It is more than that though my face has changed, it is just perfect, too perfect, every scar, crease, line and the mole that have become companions are gone, it is strange. To a friend I would look the same, but not to me. The hair is particularly weird as I started losing my hair at 16, by 20 it was gone, I could have done something about it but it seemed vain. I got a skinhead instead, now I am looking at a face in its early twenties with hair, very strange.

"So how can this be, am I a clone or the original?"

"You didn't tell him?" Dr. Moon's voice is angry as she faces the Colonel.

"He is a soldier, he takes orders, we don't DO discussions." Retorts the Colonel. Dr. Moon looks at me with some sympathy, it crosses my mind that she would make a good nurse.

"Come with me, I'll buy you a coffee."

We wander, without talking, through to the cafeteria and order a couple of coffees.

She looks me straight in the eyes.

"I've seen your reports, you're an intelligent man, why do you do what you do?"

I simply say, "I am good at it."

"But how do you stand the Bullshit?"

"When I first joined up my Colour Sergeant's first words were. 'Learn these three things and you will go far: one: You're expendable, two: It's not fair, three: You're mushrooms, they will keep you in the dark and feed you shit'. He was right, once you had that mastered these three things everything became a lot easier."

She says she understood but doesn't. Our eyes meet for a long moment, hers are deep and very caring. She takes a deep breath.

"The genetic sampling is destructive, put it another way Lance was blasted into a couple of million pieces, you should have been told."

She pauses and sighs. "I am not religious, one moment I died, the next I was alive again, younger, better than before, for me, it was not a sacrifice, but an opportunity to continue my work for another 50 years or if some of Professor Cross's changes work, another 150. The greatest sacrifice was for Professor Cross, she believes in a soul. When she stepped into the chamber she went to her death, she is still struggling with it now, before this is over there will be many questions asked of us."

I've been gifted in my life that I can avoid worrying unduly about something I cannot change; regardless of whether I am dead or not, there is not a jot I can do about it, I am like the doctor said – Younger and better than before. The Colonel knew I would step into that machine anyway, he has saved me a lot of anguish and despite his matter of fact comments, he will carry that decision for the rest of his life. To the doctor I just say

"Thanks" and meant it.

That evening a party had been arranged for us to celebrate the success of the mission. It had been the culmination of several immense technical challenges. For the project to work there were probably a million technical problems that needed to be overcome, but it was the key achievements that really impressed. Dr. Moon's team had estimated exactly the time, position and duration of the Vortex, even more impressive was the first complete cloning of a human, something quite unprecedented. The media were hailing Dr. Moon's efforts as 'The greatest technical achievement ever' and the complexity as 'like painting a masterpiece in the dark'. Dr. Moon was undoubtedly the scientist of her generation and perhaps the greatest scientist ever and ever is a very long time.

With a news story this big even the media had been overwhelmed: scientific achievement, courage, clones, colonization, space travel and all fronted by a team good enough looking to be in this week's boy or girl band. But Dr. Moon stole the whole show with her pin-up good looks, maturity and wit. The rest of us decided the best option was to get drunk and the small hours found Wolf, Cross and me slumped around a small table. It was odd that although we did not know each other particularly well, we all shared a bond, almost as if we remembered all those times when a clone would help another. Professor Cross particularly, looked at me and Wolf almost with a brotherly affection, I suppose she was aware that our role was to protect her, something I felt obliged to do even on my own planet. Then suddenly she bursts into tears and is quite inconsolable. Remembering Dr. Moon's words I clumsily try to comfort her.

"I know you believe that you have lost your soul but you haven't, you are the same person you were before."

"It's not that," she sobs, "I have a family, I Love them! I will miss them."

"Well I am sure your husband is over the moon with the new you", then I said with a little less confidence, "What do you mean you are going to miss them?"

"Right now I have one million 'mes' out there, when the first one wakes up, where will my family be?"

"They will be safe here with you," I say not really understanding where she is going with this.

"Yes, but for that me they won't be, that me will have no family, they may have years without seeing my children – they may not ever make it back!"

Lazlo Wolf, from over his glass says,

"Dr. Moon said that time can be distorted and that it takes years to land on a planet, even if we make it back, everyone we know will probably be dead."

"You see Lance," Professor Cross continues, "it's not us that have made a sacrifice, it is the others who have paid the price."

Wolf looks at her.

"You should worry more about here and now, we have all had a new lease of life, we should enjoy it." Then trying to change the subject. "What do you think we will find out there, will the planets be big empty versions of our own?"

For a moment she puffs up as if she has been paid a compliment. "Have you not read my book......... No, of course you haven't." She sighs, but then a childish smile spreads across her face, she takes another swig of her drink and gleefully launches into one of her favourite subjects.

"I am not only here because of my genealogy skills, I also wrote the de facto book on Xenology and much of this scheme we are all involved in now is based on that book. The book is based on three fundamental concepts, maths, a missing link and infinity. Let's take maths first. Lance, you are very skilled at hiding your intelligence, what's two add two?"

I rise to the compliment until I realise that she was really saying that I look like an idiot. Wolf is smiling. Sulking I say, "Four."

"Bravo Lance, top of the class and it will always be four. Just as all the things around us will always be, water will always freeze in winter, the sun will always shine in the summer and the leaves will fall off the trees in autumn. Nature is a very good designer and builds things that work, these solutions don't change or vary, because they are the optimum design for life."

Lazlo is intrigued, "So what you're saying is that there will be horses and cows and dogs and cats on these planets?"

"Well, not exactly, but close enough, in the three millennia that we have had science, we are yet to find, fake or manufacture any life forms except those based on the hydrocarbon genetic twin helix."

"Yeah!" I say nodding knowingly, "I was with you all the way until the hydro bargain getics twin horlicks bit." But she doesn't bite, she smiles, takes yet another swig and carries on.

"So much for the maths, now the missing link bit. I said that everything is based on the pretty standard gene, each group of animals shares most of its gene pattern with the others, so a Lion and Tiger have a 99% gene match. The differences are made up from variations on the same code, so a lion might be 1.1.1.2 and a tiger might be 1.1.2.1, the same but different. Now it is a fact that all life has these variations on the theme, except one, have a guess?"

Both Lazlo and me say in chorus "Humans."

"That's right, we have a tiny part of the gene that appears in no other living thing on this planet and the only reason that could be the case is.......?"

Well, sadly Lazlo and me are not that bright, or at least not that sober.

She shakes her head and just like a school teacher she taps in rhythm on our heads as she says the words, "Because .... We ....

Are …. From … Another … Planet! It, therefore, follows that if we are from another planet our ancestors must have travelled the stars and we are more than likely on lots of planets." She takes another drink. "And that brings me nicely to my last point, Infinity. There are an infinite number of planets out there and we could hit one million of them, I predict that we will hit planets, filled with animals and with humans at one phase of our history or another." With these triumphant words, she empties the last half of her glass.

Lazlo and I look at each other and smile, somehow things seem a little less scary for our clones, even if they cannot make it back, they might live out their life on a world like ours, with other people on it.

Cross is on the verge of passing out with the alcohol. She stares intensely at Wolf and then at me. It is a poor effort at a serious look, then from nowhere her face cracks into a broad smile.

"I've got a secret!" Her face is like that of a six-year-old girl teasing a friend.

"Dr. Bloody Almighty Moon is not the only genius here."

This intrigues me and Wolf, "Go on then", I say. We both edge forward like conspirators hatching a plan.

"I'll show you", she says, looking around theatrically to see if she might be overheard. She lifts her hand, took the middle finger and bends it back, almost double.

"Is that it?" Says a disappointed Wolf.

I concede, "So you are double jointed, so what?"

With some difficulty, she puts a finger over her mouth, "Shhhh."

She puts her arms around our necks and pulls us closer, so close that our heads are touching. I can smell the alcohol on her breath.

She whispers, "Yes, I am double jointed, but I wasn't!"

She pauses, but Wolf and I look at each other, whatever she is talking about, we do not get it; but slowly it sinks in, she sees this and starts nodding her head vigorously, smiling.

"Who's the Momma?" and she means it, quite literally, she has altered her DNA to make herself double jointed.

"Who is the genius now, who has been cooking in God's kitchen?"

Wolf is showing real interest, "What else have you done?"

Then like a scared kid, again she looks around,

"Don't tell Dr. Moon, she said I shouldn't do it, she said it was too dangerous, but I knew better."

"What have you done?" I am starting to get worried.

"Well, do you think Moon and I had such great tits as these before, I don't think so." She pushes her shapely chest forward. "I have done other things in some of the models, blonde, brunette, black hair, different noses, different eyes and I have done it to you three as well."

Wolf is ecstatically still focussing on Cross's chest, until he hears that she has been playing with his body as well,

"You are taking the piss!"

"Ah," she says, "And talking of piss," she continues, "do you think that I would get marooned on a planet in space with two men and not make sure I could be satisfied?"

Again Wolf and I look dumbfounded at each other,

"Ah," she giggles, "You've not noticed yet. Have another look at my tits and you will!"

But before we can take her up on the offer, suddenly, her mood changes again.

"I did all sorts, we are stronger, quicker and more intelligent than we were and we will live longer, much longer. But one thing I only did to me, I turned on my third eye, the part of the brain that we never use. And now I can hear, I can hear everybody's thoughts, it's a continuous racket, petty thoughts, vulgar thoughts and I can't stand it, which is why I am getting drunk."

With that she picks up my glass and downs it in one; then slumps down unconscious after her copious intake of alcohol.

Wolf looks at me.

"Do you think she meant it?"

"Naa, she's pissed!"

Wolf grabs his crotch, "My cock feels bigger."

"Of course it does, you are turned on looking at me!"

"Fuck off." He grins.

So that is how Wolf and I react to the news that a member of the human race has just made the most important evolutionary step since speech. We sit for a moment, pondering it, then Lazlo looks up with his wolfish grin,

"Do you know why you are on this trip?"

He waits for the optimum comedy punch line delay.

"You're a software upgrade!" He then bursts uncontrollably into a very theatrical but contagious laugh.

"How do you like that, that's why it was so rushed, at the last minute they decided they could take four not three human gene models. Though from what I heard, some of the machines were programmed without your model, you know, before you were available. Did you hear about the tests?"

I shake my head from side to side, slowly, as the alcohol is really starting to take effect.

"Yeah, they reckon that about 10% of the machines won't be able to use all the gene models anyway, something to do with data corruption; they are not sure whether we will come out like deformed monsters or whether the computer will realise and not build us. Anyway, the good news is, for me at least, is that somewhere out there in the stars there are hundreds of planets with just me and two lovely ladies and no competition from you."

He smiles, "Anyway come on help me get the Professor to bed, then you can go and talk to Your Dr. Moon."

"What do you mean 'Your Dr. Moon'?"

He winks at me, then again falls about laughing. Damn was it that obvious?

The Roof

Wolf had, with some difficulty, escaped from the confines of the store room. Below the loading hatch was the ship's superstructure, hidden behind the ships cloth covering. By cutting through this he was able to crawl under the deck level floors. It was very uncomfortable for him as he must hold on, upside down, to the ship's structure, with only the cloth between him and a fall to certain death. He managed to get below the grid of the main service corridor. This was nerve wracking as he had no space to move, detection would have meant death. He worked his way to the stern and with the ship's curvature, which the corridors followed he was able to climb out from below into the corridor, without being seen by the machine gun troops. He took with him only a pistol and a dagger. He moved to the far stern of the ship and found two shafts, one leading up and one down. He chose down, this took him to a small room, glass windows at one end. As he entered the room he realised he was down below the whole ship, probably in the fin. It was the first good look he had had of the ship. It was beautiful, huge, floating over a dark blue sea. He could see engines with propellers, driving the ship. Forwards he could see the gondola with crew moving about within. He noted that he had a complete set of the ship's controls here, this might be useful he thought.

He then came forward to the second vertical shaft leading up. He started to climb, he hoped to come out at the top of the ship above where the X10 was stored. As he reached the top he paused, his sixth sense that had saved him so many times before was in overdrive. He took the quickest of looks at the top of the ship, four men, two coming towards him, the other two seemed to be working. The nearest two were undoubtedly coming to the shaft he was in. He looked down, it was 30 paces or more, he

133

would not make it and if he was caught on the ladder they could shoot him at will. He had wanted to avoid confrontation, now he had no choice he must attack.

Wolf paused at the top of the ladders, he hunched his body up on one of the highest rungs, ready to leap onto the top of the roof. A face appeared above him, suddenly filled with shock, a split second later it was filled by the fist of Wolf. The man collapsed and fell to one side and Wolf leaped onto the roof. The other man turned and fled as did the two workmen. Wolf looked around, the ship was above cloud level and he could see its huge size stretching forward and aft. It was cylindrical like a huge cigar. It was so large that where he stood there was only a slight curve, as he looked to his side, he could see the ship fall away more and more steeply.

Then he noticed that the man he had struck was still rolling, slowly down that curve. As he watched the man rolled and slid, then suddenly with a jerk of consciousness the man flattened himself desperate to stop the fall. The man looked up.

"For God sake, help me." though the words meant nothing to Wolf the meaning was obvious. Wolf was not the killer that Lance was, he had lived his life, a hard life, living within nature. He killed, but only for his own survival or for food; even when he had become a guide for the rich and famous, it was only to raise money and political clout to keep the wild, truly wild. To see a fellow man die, needlessly, he could not do. Wolf looked about quickly and spotted the guide ropes running along the top of the ship. Quickly he loped along the walkway on top of the ship. The guide rope was tied to an eyelet at the top of the ladder, he estimated the length of rope needed and pulled out his knife. Cutting the rope he quickly made a loop on the end and threaded it around his arm, he still was not using his new hand. He then ran and swung in a large curve to where the man lay prostrate. His judgment of the rope had been perfect and he swung directly towards him, but he had misjudged the curve and he came fast, much too fast. He grabbed the man's arm but then his body swung through the other man knocking him across and down the side of the ship. Still with too much energy Wolf continued to swing moving back up the ship and lost his grip of the man. Both men desperately pawed the air trying to re-establish that hold but it was no good. The man was now another two paces down the ship desperately trying to lay still.

Wolf swung back again, but the return swing was weak and he was able to stop just above the man. Wolf, still with one arm in the rope, tried to reach with his other hand but was the breath of his hand away. The other man cursed.

Wolf, with a lifetime of necessity, was resourceful and quickly stripped away his mask, holding tightly to one end, it gave him the extra reach. He stretched again, flicking the mask at the man's hand. The other gratefully grasped it and moments later both men were firmly holding on the rope. They clambered to their feet, ready to walk up the side of the ship, like a climber would climb a steep hill. The rescued man looked relieved to see that one of the so-called demons was really a man. He extended a hand,

"Lazenby"

The sentiment was obvious in any language, Wolf warmly grasped the hand

"Wolf"

Both men warmly smiled at each other. Lazenby broad smile echoed by that of Wolf, but then Wolf stopped smiling. As Lazenby watched in horror, Wolf's face erupted from right to left, blood boiling out, then almost instantaneously Lazenby heard the crack of the rifle. He turned to see a Young Eckner cocking his weapon only 20 or 30 paces away. By the time his eyes came back to look at the man who had saved his life, Wolf was dead.

"Nooooo!" he cried aloud to the world.

There was nobody else on the top of the Hindenburg, the other workers had fled. In a split second, Lazenby knew that he must kill this murderer. Whether it was his outrage of seeing a man, for a man it was, being so needlessly gunned down. Whether deep in his mind he saw the opportunity to kill this enemy spy and get the book. Maybe it was his self-preservation, for surely the other spy would be thinking the same. He started to sprint towards his opponent, though he knew he would never make it.

Here amongst the clouds, two men were about to wage war, literally on top of the world. These two men were alike, so alike and yet each saw the other as the enemy. Both were men of action, brave men, good men, but they stood for different anthems.

Young Eckner watched surprised for a moment as Lazenby screamed and charged at him. He knew he was a British spy, but he had just saved his life by killing the creature. He paused a moment, then made his decision, Lazenby had cast his dice, there could be only one winner. He quickly tried to complete cocking the rifle but in his haste, he jammed the breach. He looked up. Lazenby was nearly on him. He wiggled the cocking handle it wouldn't move, again Lazenby was closer. Young Eckner was no soldier, he wiggled the handle again, suddenly it slid back into place, no time to shoulder the weapon, he fired from the hip.

Bang!

Lazenby felt no pain, then almost instantly he was on Young Eckner, he struck him full force in his face with his forearm. Blood exploded from Young Eckner's mouth but Lazenby had come at a charge and his whole body flew into Young Eckner, winding him and knocking him clear off his feet. The two landed with Lazenby on top, but Young Eckner immediately rolled him off, the two tumbled down the ever steepening roof of the Hindenburg. Eventually they stopped, Young Eckner pulled a knife from his belt. He clearly had the upper hand, but he is not a killer, Lazenby was. Each man held the right arm of his opponent in his own left. Again they rolled towards the ever closer chasm of the side of the ship, Lazenby launched his head at Young Eckner's mouth. His teeth shattered, some even cut through his lip, but he spat them at Lazenby and the two fought on. Young

Eckner rolled Lazenby off but as he too is rolled the two temporarily lost contact. It was only then that they realised that they had passed the point of no return. Both men forgot the fight and each focused only on their will to live. Lazenby flattened himself to the ship's roof, he was two paces higher up the ship's side than Young Eckner, who desperately tried to grab for his ankle, all he got was a boot in his face. He slid another two paces down. Lazenby, not a minute earlier was here, fighting for his life, he took a breath and slowly started to crawl back to safety, meticulously placing one arm at a time, then one foot and moving only a couple of centimetres. Slowly he edged his way back to safety. Young Eckner, too, slowly lifted his hand to gain those couple of centimetres, but as he brought his hand down he slid another half a pace down. Again, he lifted his hand and again he slid, but this time, even when he put his hand down, he did not stop sliding. His movement was imperceptible but he was moving closer and closer to the steeper and steeper side and the inevitable fall from the ship. As a last desperate surge, he tried to swim up the ship, flailing his arms and legs, but it just accelerated him towards the edge. The irony of a great climber falling from the top of the world was not lost on Lazenby. Young Eckner looked Lazenby straight in the eye.

"Why?" he said, then he is gone. Lazenby did not hear a scream.

The Attack

Eckner burst into the officers' mess.

"It's on the top fighting, let's try and rush that Scorpion and get it out of the hatch."

Schumann immediately leapt into action, his weapon was already cocked and he was summoning his men. A few quick words for his assembled men.

"Check magazines, pouches and safety off." He said mechanically, like a mantra, his men did not need any reminders.

Eckner shouted, "Come on," and took off down the corridor, the two of them had already discussed this situation and Schumann, ever thorough, had briefed his men. Two men remained in position on the MP34 heavy machine gun, four plus Eckner and Schumann darted forward. Their plan was simple if they got a chance to get into the store room if the Scorpion was dormant, get the winch on it and lift it above the trap door and drop it into the ocean. The surprise encounter on top of the ship gave them the ideal opportunity.

"Watch for Blenkinsopp." Schumann shouted to his men.

"Blenkinsopp? Where is he?" said Eckner.

"There he is Sir" as Blenkinsopp ran into the corridor shouting and waving his arms in the air.

"No, No, No!"

Involuntarily those with weapons raised them, when Lance followed into the corridor, weapon in arms, the youngest trooper fired. Few people can separate the brain from the body, when things happen quickly. When running, you respond quickly.

Trooper Rolf was only 19, he loved his family, they loved him, they were proud when he joined the army, prouder still when he joined the elite German ski troops. He was a good soldier and a good Christian. He fired responsively at the demon, in a blink ten rounds went down the corridor, three found Blenkinsopp, none found the demon. The demon, however, a veteran of more battles than all his enemies put together, fired decisively, a double tap, he played the percentage shot, his Colonel had told him "Put the man down, shoot for the middle of the torso", the second shot was insurance. His first round found the mark, trooper Rolf, a hit a hands width above his navel, the weapon recoiled high, the second shot was high, Rolf right cheek bone erupted, he was dead before he hit the floor.

They were in a dance of death, to the pounding rhythm of their hearts, a provocation, a reaction, a counter reaction. The smoke slowly spiralled from Lance's weapon, he was kneeling in a prayer like position, perhaps even offering a prayer to his god of death. He waited, he regrouped, he knew, it was inevitable, it was the thunder to his lightning, five men reacted, Schumann the only rock in a storm screaming

"No!" as he hit the deck, "No! Hold your fire!"

His voice was drowned as one hundred rounds rang down the corridor, twenty-eight replied. Any who were standing died, Eckner only survived as the bloodied flying body of the trooper in front somersaulted into him, knocking him flat, unconscious on the floor. Even those rounds that missed a man, injured the already damaged Hindenburg. Schumann was equal to his task, his men had foolishly fired, but he would revenge their death.

Lance had nowhere to go, marooned two paces forward from the doorway he had only seconds earlier left, he lay rolling, changing the magazine on a weapon he was not familiar with, a technology he was not familiar with. Schumann took aim and laid down punishingly accurate fire, he had lived his life for this moment.

Red flashes burst across Lance's head and shoulders.

* * * * * * * * * * * * * * * * ** * * * * * *** * * * *

"Shit! Move, Move, Move!" My arms fly up instantly, it is hard, unless you train, you naturally cover up when people shoot at you. I roll, left and right, but he is hitting, he is good. A few more hits and the shield will fail, then my weapon explodes into pieces as it is hit by a round. Must make it back to the store room, protect the X10. Suddenly the fire stops, I look up, he is changing magazine, of the thirty rounds that he has fired twenty have hit. Shit! Time to go. I stand up turn and run for the door. Then they hit me, the large calibre weapon's deep blat, blat, blat, strike me in the back, my shield is almost gone, the energy from the rounds cart-wheels me past the door, I go with it, I have too. Run! I dodge, another hit, roll, swoop, keep going, I cover maybe 50 paces, I find a service shaft in the floor and dive into it. Bad idea, it plunges down to the bottom of the ship, I just catch the top rung but the force pops my shoulder. I can't hold on, I bounce down the shaft, grabbing what I can with my other arm, I land on my dislocated shoulder. I have experienced a lot of pain before, all sorts of pain. This pain, how do you describe it? It was white hot, I am fighting another losing battle with consciousness, I have failed. It's down to Wolf now. I black out.

* * * * ** * * * * * * * * * * * * ** * * * * * * * * * * * * *

As the smoke cleared from the service corridor Schumann could see no demon.

"I'll go and finish it off Sir", He was already on his feet in pursuit of Lance.

"No! Wait. We have no time, let's take care of the Scorpion. Schumann, secure the site and send a runner to get more men."

Within five minutes the efficient German crew and troopers had cleared away the ever rising number of dead bodies. Blenkinsopp was mortally wounded, three rounds had hit him, two in the leg which were not too serious. The other however was a stomach shot, he would slowly bleed to death. They propped him up against wall, his life force oozed slowly out between his fingers as he tried to hold his stomach, though he knew it would not help. All he had achieved in life was little more than a carcass sitting in a crimson puddle. The indomitable Blenkinsopp was not through though, he had risked his life to stop this destruction, he would die for that effort; but not yet. He was desperately trying to talk but could form no coherent words. He had only a few minutes left in this world.

Eckner meanwhile had two of the crew lashing the winch rope to the X10.

"Start the winch" he shouted.

The still inactive X10 was dragged along the floor to the winch where it was lifted into the air, above the stout trap door. Eckner could see the kaleidoscope of colour in its abdomen and realised that this must be another birth.

"Not on my ship!" he shouted aloud. The crew turned, realised it was not an order to them and carried on.

"Open the trap door!"

The large trap door was pulled back, revealing a dark night and far below a dark angry sea. A push on the winch lock and the X10 would drop to oblivion.

Kruger appeared at the door, he had been noticeable by his absence, while others fought and died. He ran to the scorpion, paused as he neared it, kicked it and then moved to its tail.

"This belongs to the Fuhrer" he shouted as started to tug at the Key of Solomon still spiked by the scorpion's tail.

"Kruger, stand back, we are going to drop that beast."

"Not, with the book, the Fürher wants this book, he needs this book." That was enough for the crew, no sane person would actively disobey a highly placed Nazi when he mentioned Hitler. Eckner was not impressed though.

"Kruger, that beast will drop with or without you, it's your choice."

"Stop!" Shouted Lazenby. It had taken some time to traverse back across the roof of the Hindenburg, as he ran up the corridor his quick eyes had taken account of the events. He had paused for a moment with his friend Blenkinsopp. He had not realised how close he had become to this fat American until now, as he looked down at him dying. Lazenby had seen wounds like this before, he knew Blenkinsopp had only minutes with the living. His eyes looked at Lazenby, he was trying to speak, but his eyes said it all.

"I know. You were right! I will try and stop them, God bless, my friend"

With that Blenkinsopp had done his work, he could trust his friend to take up the fight, he had the faintest smile on his lips, his hands went limp and he passed out.

Lazenby ran into the store room. He saw the trap door open, he saw the Scorpion dangling precariously over the precipice, Kruger still tugging at the book.

"Stop!" He shouted.

Lazenby was always a man of action, not words, he dived forward and leaped on the machine.

"Are you mad? Stand back, are you both mad!" screamed Eckner.

"They are not evil, the creature tried to save me."

"That demon just killed four more men, your friend Blenkinsopp included."

"I don't believe you, I cannot let you destroy them."

"Sailor," Eckner said to the man on the winch. "I will count to five, on five you let the winch go, with or without Mr. Lazenby and Kruger."

"Aye, Sir"

"One"

Nobody moved.

"Two"

Still no movement.

"Three"

Kruger lost his nerve and backed off, Lazenby did not, but he knew Eckner would do it. Both were men of honour and responsibility.

"Four"

But Lazenby's responsibility was to King and country not an alien – he prepared to leap off when it was released.

"Captain." It was the executive officer.

Eckner paused for a moment. He would have gone to five, but his XO was a good man and would not interrupt unless it was important. He turned to the XO.

"What is it?" He tried to mask the tension in his voice.

"Sir, number three and four bags are ruptured, we are losing altitude quickly, there is a Loch ten minutes away. I suggest we land and make repairs there." He said this in the same tone that you would ask someone if they had milk in their tea.

"Very well, I will join you on the bridge presently," he turned to back to Lazenby, "Schumann, enough of this, place Lazenby under arrest if he does not come quietly shoot him."

Schumann and one of his men forcibly removed Lazenby from the Scorpion. Kruger was still vainly, trying to get his book.

Eckner told the winch operator,

"If it moves drop it!"

Lazenby was not coming easily, until a trooper smashed the butt of his weapon into Lazenby's already bruised cheek, his cheek split open and gushed with blood. The strike knocked Lazenby flat –he was barely conscious.

"Bastard, you'll get yours!" Mumbled the disorientated Lazenby. The four men, Eckner, the XO, the Trooper dragging Lazenby, moved off up the corridor towards the bow of the ship.

Lazenby was half hauled by his guard who carried an MP38 machine gun. Lazenby had an ace up his sleeve, the guard was not used to handling prisoners. As the group neared the place he had stashed the Lugar pistol, he stumbled forward. As he expected the guard lunged forward to keep a hold of him, Lazenby threw his head back with all this might, it was not pretty but it worked. The guard's nose exploded across his face and he clutched at his ruined visage. Lazenby, quick as a cat, sprung for his Lugar, by the time the other three men had reacted from the surprise, they were staring at the barrel of the gun. Eckner looked for once dumbfounded.

"Don't be foolish, Lazenby. I only did what was best for the safety of the ship, no hard feelings, eh?" He thought he was dealing with an English gentleman, playing by the Queensbury rules. It had not registered yet where this gun had come from and what it was doing there.

"Eckner, I am going back and unhooking the scorpion if you follow me I will kill you."

"You will shoot me, I don't think so"

"No you are right, I won't shoot YOU, but I will shoot HIM." With total cold-heartedness which shocked Eckner, Lazenby pointed the weapon at the thigh of the guard. BANG! The guard collapsed to the floor screaming.

"Now gentlemen, I will be leaving you?"

As Lazenby walked past the prostrate trooper, he relieved him of his weapon. Almost instantly Lazenby heard the rapid steps of Schumann clanging down the corridor.

"What's happened? Where is Johansson?"

"I shot him, only a leg shot, he'll live." Said Lazenby aiming his weapon at Schumann. He pointed at Schumann's weapon and pointed at the floor, Schumann obeyed, dropping his weapon.

"You will pay for this Lazenby."

"No doubt, Schumann, but not here and not now, leave the heavy gun in place as well."

Lazenby returned back to the storage area. As he entered Kruger had a large pole and was trying to lever the book off the scorpion's tail, but he was struggling as the whole thing was swaying from the winch.

"Out!" Lazenby said in a voice that left no one in any doubt.

Moments later, all the German crew were forword, including Kruger without the book. Lazenby was trying to tend to his dying friend Blenkinsopp.

The Escape

I don't know how long I had been unconscious, but when I came too I climbed up the service ladder. It was all-quiet, so I moved carefully forward, back to the store room. As I neared I saw a man leaning over an injured Blenkinsopp. I moved more stealthily now if this man had been responsible for injuring my friend, then I would kill him. But as I neared, Blenkinsopp saw me.

"Glad you could join the party, Lance, though I don't think I will be dancing much today! This is my friend Lazenby."

I nod at Lazenby and quickly inspect Blenkinsopp's wounds,

"Let's move him back to the X10, The Scorpion!"

Lazenby shakes his head slowly,

"He'll die if we move him."

"Don't be an idiot man, he is going to die anyway and we might just join him if we stay in a corridor, besides the next birth is Dr. Moon – she might be able to help."

Lazenby grabs one arm, me the other and we drag Blenkinsopp, for a moment he weakly chastises us but then, thankfully, passes out. I have seen many injuries, this was not survivable. Most of the man's blood had congealed in a large pool around him and there was a sizable hole in his stomach. We managed to drag him through the hole in the wall and placed him on some large sacks of vegetables, they were reasonable flat and a lot more comfortable than the floor.

"Lazenby, keep an eye on the corridor, I think the X10 is near to birth."

Sure enough, almost on cue, the X10 convulses and adopts the position. Somehow, I look forward to the appearance of Dr.

Moon, she is more than just as a medical resource. She's mentally strong, confident and might make some sense out of all this nonsense, I think having a mother figure around might cheer me up. The X10 gives one final convulsion and out slides the body, but it's not Dr. Moon. Even covered in the clinging black combat suit, I can tell that this was not her, this is something out of one of my wet dreams. All I can see is slick, moist, black, curves, oh yes lots of curves and all in the right places. The combat suit seems to cling and squeeze the girls figure accentuating her body. She is laying on her back and the suit hid nothing. She rolls over and vomits, her breasts must be made of wood, as they easily fight off all attempts of gravity to move them as she sits up. Her head is facing me, my eyes travel the length of her body to her tight rounded buttocks, which are pointed directly at a dumb-founded Lazenby.

"Urhh, that was worse than I thought", she says.

"Where is Dr. Moon?" I almost sound convincing for a moment, like right now I give a damn.

"Do you think I was always old, you idiot."

"Dr. Moon?" I ask stupidly. "I er… I er… did not think anyone could be that bright AND that beautiful." Oh shit, I think, dumb bastard, corny lines are us.

She pulls herself to her feet and just for a moment looks at me,

"There might be hope for you yet, Major," then she notices the state I am in and she immediately swaps into doctor mode.

"My God, are you alright, where is Wolf."

"I am fine, these are friends" I wave my hands towards Blenkinsopp and Lazenby, "Help him, he has been shot and is losing blood fast."

Lazenby, realizing that there might be some hope for his friend, crosses the room towards her,

"He has been shot in the gut and has lost a lot of blood, can you help him?"

Dr. Moon looks at me,

"Can you understand a word of what he is saying?"

Of course, I realize that her translator is not tuned in yet, I translate for her. She immediately busies herself, feels his pulse, inspects the wound, grabs Lazenby and makes him press on the wounds.

"I have an idea, it might be too late but it is worth trying," she says moving over to the control panel of the X10. She brings up a menu I have not seen before, I watch her scrolling through a list of options, at each change a three-dimensional model appears. The first four were the team but then shapes I have never seen before appear, insect-like creatures, I can't say I liked the look of any of them. She pauses finally on a worm looking thing and hits the "Go" button.

"This is God's kitchen at work gentlemen but it will take five minutes to create."

"What the hell was that", I ask.

"You'll see."

But Lazenby is losing his fight to keep Blenkinsopp in the game,

"We're losing him, for God sake do something now!"

Dr. Moon dips under the X10 and places her hand on a panel, it momentarily lights then swings open, she reaches inside and pulls out a first aid kit. Working quickly she assembles a pressure injector, puts in a tube of drug and gives Blenkinsopp the medication. He immediately dies, or at least that is what it looks like.

"I've induced a coma, it will stop his heart pumping his blood out all over the floor, it will last long enough for the "leech" to work. But if we don't hurry his brain will die."

Lazenby looks unconvinced, I move over to the hole in the wall – it is Dr. Moon's job to put people back together, mine is to make sure it never happens in the first place, or may be to put them in that state, depending on how you see these things.

The moments stretched to seconds, seconds to minutes and what seemed like an eternity as Blenkinsopp gradually but progressively turned blue with lack of blood oxygen. Finally, the X10 births a small wriggling monster. It is about 25cm long but only the width of a straw and is more caterpillar than worm, Dr. Moon tentatively picks it up. I notice she stays well away from its head, then lowers it towards the worst of Blenkinsopp's wounds. It seems to smell the blood and becomes almost frantic, as the Doctor finally let's go it circles menacingly around the wound then plunges in. It is truly the most gut-wrenching thing I have ever seen, it practically burrows into the wound. Moments later, however, its head re-appears and it starts munching at the wound, it is only after a few moments that I realize that it is actually filling the wound, almost weaving a skin.

"What the hell was that," I ask, stomach still churning.

"It's a genetically manufactured creature that can detect injury or disease and will roam the body healing. It will exist for 24 hours before it dies, it still does not have a name, though maybe we should name it after its first patient. We need to bring him round again."

With that she unceremoniously strikes Blenkinsopp in the chest, he lurches, takes a large breath and sags back down again, though he is quite evidently alive again.

"He will be unconscious for some time and weak, the creature will repair him but cannot replace the blood, only rest will do that. Now, Major can you give me an update on how we are doing?"

It took me about five minutes to update Dr. Moon and to hear the even worse news from Lazenby that Wolf would not be coming back. It was odd though because even as he told me I didn't really care, I thought that we could just cook up another one in the Scorpion. Had this creation of Dr. Moon so devalued life?

Dr. Moon looks and me and says.

"From what you say, Lance, it looks like we need to get the X10 off this ship and somewhere a little more private while we get organized. The good news is that we are on a high-tech planet and one already inhabited by our race, it seems Professor Cross was correct in her theory. Do you have any ideas how to get us off this flying ship?"

"We can get off pretty easily," I say, "Lazenby here says that there is a small aircraft just across the corridor that he can fly but the only way to get the X10 down is by taking over the ship."

"Can we do that?"

"Well, so far we've pretty well had our ass kicked but they have taken casualties too, I think it can be done, but it's very risky. I think it's better to back off and fight another day, as you can see we are moving along the coast. We have a better chance on the ground, the terrain looks pretty rugged we should be able to hide easily. Are you absolutely sure we need the X10, I know that we did not train for this situation, but could you build the gate with what is on this planet?"

"No, this planet is 500 years behind us," she says gloomily.

"But you're not, you could help them."

"Yes, but even then it might take 50 or 100 years. We also need to think about getting their governments involved or not, we really need to weigh this up before we make any big decisions, for now, we need to keep as many of the aces up our sleeve and that includes the X10."

"OK," I say, "What I suggest we do is….."

But before I can get out my words the noise of heavy boots could be heard scraping across the metallic floor of the corridor.

"Shit, they are coming for us! Take a look Lazenby."

Lazenby cautiously pops his head out into the corridor to be greeted by the buzz and bang of automatic gunfire.

"Right, Dr. Moon at this moment you are the most important resource on this planet, let's get you out of here, I am going to stay here and try and get the X10 on the floor. Lazenby, you are going to take Blenkinsopp and Dr. Moon on the aircraft. We need a safe meeting point, where?"

Lazenby turns to me and smiles broadly.

"We could all finish up anywhere, so we should meet in London, which is our capital city, go to Oxford Street, there is a club called the 'Kat Klub', ask for me in there." He pushes out his hand, I take hold of it and he pumps it vigorously, I assume this was some sort of farewell custom.

"Good luck old boy." He says. With the help of Dr. Moon, he picks up Blenkinsopp, who was still limp. The three move to the door, Lazenby has a pistol in his right hand, I stand facing them with a machine gun in mine.

"On three, one, two, three!"

I leap out into the corridor standing tall and firing my weapon. I am trying to shield my team. I am aghast to see at least six men pointing their weapons at me.

"Go!"

I sense rather than see the three start to move behind me, Lazenby is cracking off his pistol as he staggers across, he has no chance of hitting anything but it will have a morale effect on the others. It looks like we have taken them by surprise as no shots are coming back. Rather than trying to take people out, I am more interested in spraying the general area, try to force their heads down, the nearest is probably only three or four car lengths from me. After about my twentieth round fired, I see a man drop and then it happens, they all start to fire. Bang, Bang, Bang, again I hear the reports of weapon fire, again I hear the rounds fly past me buzzing like angry bees. But this time, I make no effort to duck and dive or weave, this time, I am the armour for my team.

The first round that hits strikes my shoulder, it spins me like a top, my weapon flipping into the air, still firing. As I spin I see my team are in the room, now I can move. But already a second, third round hits me and I hit the deck. With a monumental physical effort and a lot of luck, I am flung still spinning through the door that I had only moments earlier stepped through. The game is just about up for me. I painfully crawl to the doorway and pull myself up so that I am sitting with my back against the door, but still inside the room; rounds are still buzzing down the corridor. There is an ugly sharp bump sticking up on the front of my shoulder which tells me that my clavicle has snapped and my left leg from half way down my shin has a sickening angle of about 30 degrees. Thankfully I am still seriously medicated but I know that sooner or later that it's going to hurt like hell, or at least I am hoping I'll be alive to feel the pain. As they say in the marines, 'Pain reminds you that you are still alive'. But more worrying in my mind, the mind of a soldier, is that I am now pretty well useless. What we need is time, it was time to negotiate.

"Stop firing, stop firing!"

For a moment the shots continue, then a strong voice stops them.

"Who is shouting, is that you Lazenby?"

I need some sort of ruse to confuse them, anything as long as it sounds even half-plausible, might slow them down.

"My name is Major Lance, I am a soldier, some of your crew are British spies and my team was trying to capture them."

It is the best I can do, with my limited language and even more limited knowledge of this world.

"What unit are you from Major Lance?"

All our units are named after animals, Blenkinsopp had named a few for me, so I pick one.

"The Eagles."

"What? What sort of unit is that. I've never heard of them."

Right, so the Germans don't call their units after animals. Try again.

"That's right, we are secret, nobody has heard of us." I say rather unbelievably, despite my pain I grin, they are never going to buy that.

From across the corridor comes a noisy rasping noise, as the Herschel's engine turns over.

"What is going on down there?"

"We are taking the Scorpion to pieces, it should not have attacked your men, it is dangerous."

"Who commands your unit?"

Now I was in trouble, I needed a name or a rank, neither of which could I just make up, I was about to plug for another animal – Lion, when my eye catches the label of one of the nearby beer bottles."

"Becks."

This apparently hits the mark as I could hear some low mumbling.

"Becks of the Ministry of Defence?"

I had no idea what 'Ministry of Defence' meant but, hey, when you are on a roll.

"Yeah, that's right, he works closely with the President."

"President?"

Immediately I hear men moving down the corridor, I am sure Blenkinsopp had said, President. But before I am made to pay for my error the engine on the aircraft bursts into full song.

"They are trying to escape in the plane, quick attack."

Now I am on more familiar ground, I slump around the corner and take out the first soldier who is already running down the corridor. The rest immediately hit the deck and return fire. I push myself upright and out of harm's way and feel a noticeable bump as the aircraft parts company with the ship. The engine roars away. Suddenly I feel jubilant, Dr. Moon, the babe Moon, has escaped and with her goes the best hopes of my planet.

"Not a bad day's work, rescued the planet and the damsel." I shout down the corridor in my own language.

Now without anybody else to worry about I can save my own skin and just maybe that of the X10, but just how I have no idea.

Muffled voices carry up the corridor. I for my part had kept ranting in several languages, including my own, just to unnerve them and maybe even make them think that there was more than just me. They probably thought that I could not hear them but I could.

"Schumann, we are landing any minute now in Loch Ness, we must make a move."

"But Sir, he knows what he is doing, he has killed two of my men trying to rush him."

"In five minutes we will have the Royal Navy crawling all over this ship, I don't want an armed demon on board at that time. Do I make myself clear?"

"Yes, Sir."

I decide it is time to move. The ship has progressively descended and I can clearly see the waves on the water below, we are on a long but quite narrow estuary. If landed on the ground I might be able to let the winch go and escape on the X10. It is a long shot, a very long shot, but it is the only one I have.

I crawl onto the X10 and strap myself onto its back, this is very dangerous in my state as the hatch is already open. How comical I must look, a beat up, drugged up soldier, riding a scorpion with a book stuck to its tail. All I need to do is take the brake off the winch and I will slide to the earth. I lay there, piggybacking this metallic monster.

I can hear them moving down the corridor, slowly, progressively, like the tide moving up a beach. Then there is silence.

The first soldier bursts around the corner, weapon blazing, he is easy, I put a bullet in his forehead. The next is rolling, harder, it takes three rounds before he is stopped and then my weapon stops. No more rounds, no more time.

There are several soldiers in the room, they have bobbed and rolled and found a place from which to fire. One of them stands up, confidently, as if he is going to offer me his seat, he is smiling.

"You are a strong warrior my friend, for that your death will be quick."

"Wait!" A man steps forward holding a pistol, he is no soldier, though he wears a uniform.

He raises his weapon and points it between my eyes.

"My name is Kruger, SS, it would be rude to kill a stranger", he leans forward and pulls the mask off my face.

"Ah, as I thought, you are not a demon but what or who are you?"

I glance below me, we are only a building's height above the surface of a choppy sea.

"What am I, I am gone!"

With that, I slap the lever on the hook which holds the X10. It immediately opens and I plummet down, strapped still to the back of the monster. I hear the report of a weapon, but he is too slow, I am already dropping, but as the Scorpion begins to fall the extra weight at its front forces it to rotate, its tail whips forward, straight through the chest of Kruger. Despite its weight, the Scorpion jolts, held for a moment by the man. In that split second I look up, he stands there amazed, staring at the spike, as thick as my arm, in his chest. Pushed against his chest is a book that had been impaled early. Oddly, he seems to realize what the book is and lifts his arms to embrace it, smiling, but then his legs buckle and, him, the scorpion and me riding bareback fall into the void.

I hit the water with a crushing shock, which is doubled by the breath-taking chill of the sea as it surrounds me. The impact robs my lungs of what air they had and my body spasms with the cold. Even as my head goes under water my lungs are bursting for air, air which I cannot get. I am on a one-way roller coaster ride to the bottom of the sea. I am strapped akimbo on the back of a large lump of metal. I sink like a brick. Almost instantly my ears erupt in pain, I can feel the pressure on my chest, I fumble for the rope which binds me to my watery coffin. I am dying.

The Epilogue

A newsman stands clutching a large microphone, standing in front of a camera. The large boat rolls as it rides the small swell, either due to the movement of the boat or perhaps the previous night's Scottish hospitality, the reporter looks a little grey. As a true professional he looks mournfully at the camera and says;

"Ok," then bursts into his best smile as the camera rolls.

"There is no more famous a monster than the Loch Ness monster or just Nessie as the locals call her. And here we have this year's first expedition trying to find her but this time, it's different. This is the best-funded search of all-time and comes with "BOB" a large fast submersible with its own sonar. This summer we will know once and for all whether Nessie is fact or fiction. Anthony Baines on Loch Ness for the BBC."

Meanwhile inside.

"We are coming up on it now," say the young pilot.

The group of people all look intensely into the colour monitor at a grey expanse. The pilot smoothly moves his controls as he too watches the monitor.

"I can't make it out, I can see several tubes sticking out."

"Don't worry young man," says the women with an air of confidence, "it is a German weapon used in World War II, it never worked, it looks like a giant scorpion. Get it slung under BOB and let's bring it up into the airlock."

It is more than half a century since the events of the Hindenburg's ditching. Looking at the papers of the day would reveal how the Hindenburg had a Jewish stowaway, who enraged by disease, had killed several of the crew. How the Captain with the assistance of the Royal Navy was able to secure all the passengers without mishap. The Nazi propaganda machine had rolled into full effect and the story was out on the front pages for a couple of days, unlike the events so soon afterwards when the Hindenburg burst into flames in a routine docking in the USA.

Of those who took part in the events few survived and with no evidence; what were they to say anyway? Eckner was soon retired and Schumann had wars to fight; first a civil war in Spain, then a World War, where he died on the Russian front. As for the mission, it could not be completed without the advanced technologies inside the X10. Though the last half of the 20th century has seen an unprecedented advance in physics, astronomy, genetics and particularly in computing. This explosion of technology has sometimes been too fast, like splitting the atom, a necessary evil to end a World War. The author of these events has managed to stay anonymous, carefully planting the seeds of knowledge with the greatest minds of our time.

I turn around to a woman now 70 years old, though technically she was 25 when born so that makes her nearly 100, she looks less than forty. I must marry here someday.

Ian Anderton was practically tap dancing, he said quietly,

"Do you expect me to believe that crock of shite? That ain't no German weapon, Gregory"

"I know, patience!" I said, "Come on we'll go down to the airlock."

A few minutes later we are stood in the airlock of the ship, the room is filled with the hissing of compressed air. In the centre is a large hole, with 200 meters of the loch water below. The surface starts to seethe and then takes on a yellow hue, as BOB emerges. It is an impressive piece of hardware, about the size of a large car, bright yellow, with an array of lights, arms and sensors. One of the crew leaps onto its relatively level back and hooks up the hoists front and back.

"OK," I say, "everybody out, we need to check its stable before we can stow it." I lie but we don't need the entire crew to see this quite yet.

Anderton looks at me, with that 'you can't mean me' look on his face.

"You can stay Anderton, but you'll owe me."

He beams enthusiastically.

With that, I press the green button on my control and the whole thing starts to rise into the air. As BOB clears the surface a darker form underneath comes into view. The X10 is still pristine with not a trace of rust, though covered in silt. Anderton is stunned.

I spin the X10 round, it is easy to manoeuvre slung as it is. I check the tail, still impaled on it is the skeletal remains of Kruger and the book. With little ceremony or care I take a sweeping brush and smash the bones of Kruger, he slides back into the Loch and disappears. He deserves no more, he was an evil man who came to an evil end. I then slide the book off the spike. It is in remarkably good shape, probably due to the lack of oxygen at the muddy bottom of the Loch. I turn to Anderton and tap the X10.

"This I cannot tell you about, not yet!"

Dr. Moon continues. "No Mr. Anderton, not yet, but you realise that we could have kept the whole thing from you."

Anderton looks confused, but not angry, "So why did you show it to me if you don't want me to report it."

Dr. Moon smiles, "Because, very soon, we will need you to help us tell a much bigger story."

"But for now," I say, "you might like to write about this." I hold up the book, I go to throw it but then stop. "Before I give you this, I should say that everyone who has come into contact with it has died"

"We all die, Gregory. I'll write about your book and I'll wait for the big story, but first tell me what your real name is, Gregory."

159

"Me?" I laugh, "Major Lance at your service."

It has been seventy years, but soon we will complete our mission, I wonder how the other one million 'mes' got on, it will be interesting to meet them! But first, we will be inviting Lazlo Wolf and Professor Cross for dinner, once we have grown them, of course.

Chapter 1 of Shadow Warrior

"Fuck!" I break the surface of the water and my burning lungs take their first gasp of air. My body mechanically pumps huge drafts into my lungs as I desperately try to get my breath. With each, I spit the salty water that sprays into my face. It's only then that I notice the extreme cold, nearly on top of my breathing I challenge the gods, or fate or whatever got me here.

"Shit."

I look around, it's dark, I try to work out where I am, I've no idea how I got here. I am bouncing up and down in some red liquid. NO. I am in the sea, it's the swell of the water that's moving me and the odd wave that is covering me in salty foam.

"So what all this red?" I ask no one in particular.

Whatever it is, it's not good, I think it's blood. I quickly check myself out, see if it's mine. I lift my arms and legs, run my freezing hands over my body. I am wearing a black combat suit, but I seem to be in good shape, the blood's not mine. I rub my hands over my head.

"Ouch!" I find a sore part, look at my fingers, sure there is blood, but not enough for what I am in, there must be a bucket full to make the red slick that I am in. It then occurs to me that treading water in a bloody pool in the sea is a really bad idea, it's time to move. I roll over onto my face and start to do the front crawl. I am a pretty good swimmer, but I usually have goggles, I can't put my face in the water, not this water anyway, so I swim with my head up, it's uncomfortable. As I am looking forward I rise on swell and see some land, maybe only the length of a football pitch away, it's dark I can't make out how big it is. I can only see the white foam as it crashes onto the rocks. That's got to be better than here so I strike out for it. I reckon I could normally do 100m in one minute thirty, but in a swell, with no goggles, I am not sure. So I take my time.

Then I see it, something big in the water on my left, really big, really fucking enormously big. My brain is telling me that it looks big because I am in the water and I am low, but it still looks bloody big. I only catch a glimpse, it's black, I see a large white patch and it's got a huge dorsal fin. It must be eight paces long. I change my mind about taking my time, I kick like crazy and go for the rocks. I stick my face into the water, for better speed, foolishly I open my eyes, its darker with my eyes open than shut, it freaks me out. I can see nothing, how deep is this water, what's beneath me? I am stroking hard now, my brain desperately tries to coach my body, the brain says long powerful strokes, clean entry, grab the water, pull to your groin and push the hands back out past your thigh; but my body just tries to move the arms as fast as they can go, that means short useless strokes.

The black shape moves up behind me, I catch a glimpse of it only 10m behind me. I redouble my efforts, I actually feel the water rushing by me, then I realise that I am actually being pushed by the huge bulk of the water that the thing is displacing, it must be right on my feet now. I mentally brace myself for the attack, but the next pain I feel is in my hands as it smashes into shell encrusted rock. I feel a huge surge of water behind me and I desperately drag myself over the submerged rock. I turn just in time to see a mouth the size of a car boot smash closed a hand's breadth in front of my face. The creature turns to one side, a jet black, but intelligent eye looks straight into mine for a long moment, then it kicks a huge tail and it is gone under the sea.

I turn back to face the shore and am immediately hit from the side by a wave that bounces me back over the rock and again into the deep sea. I frantically kick and scramble, not to lose hold of the rock, but suddenly it's gone. I am again treading water in deep water. I drive for the rock again, arms and feet wind-milling desperately to get out of the deep water and away from the monster, that must surely bite any moment. But for a second time I reach the rock, this time, I bowl straight over, striking for the rocks in front. Again, a second wave hits, this time, I am past the rock so it cannot wash me to sea, but instead it smashes me against a rock, a rock covered with the shells of molluscs. Each shell slices across my back. Luckily the combat suit takes most of the hit, but another wave follows, then another. I play a frantic and exhausting game of snakes and ladders. In between the waves I launch forward scrabbling over a rock or two; then a wave crashes. If I'm lucky I stay where I am and get cut up on the rock as the vice like wave presses me into the cheese grater surface. If I am unlucky I snake back two or three rocks and get cut up even more. For a full half an hour I play this desperate game until finally I get beyond the rocks and find smooth water, ten steps later I find a sandy beach. There I collapse bleeding from hands and feet, knees and elbows, back and chest, my clothes are in shreds, my skin in tatters. I am bewildered and I have no idea where I am or what I was doing and right now I couldn't care less. I collapse on the sand and drive my hands into it, then I pass out.

At dawn, I wake up shivering. I lift my head and the muscles of my neck scream. I roll over onto my back and wince as the salty sand comes into contact with my torn back. I've been here before, this level of pain I can take and I know it. I stand up. The world spins for a moment but then comes back into focus. I have a deep, angry pain in my forehead, I think I am concussed, but…

"I'm alive!" I shout.

I stand there for a moment and try and put it together. I know who I am, I am Major Lance, a marine and I am pretty sure I am on a mission, but what mission I have no idea. I remember the water from last night and the blood, somehow I finished up in the water. Maybe I was in a plane crash? Either way with that thing swimming around out there I am not going back in the water. I remember the head wound, maybe that is why I can't remember. But however I got here I am now in a survival situation. I need water, food and shelter, then we will see. I look around, where am I. I notice it's pretty cold, must be high in the northern or southern hemisphere, it's not arctic but it's not far off. I again start to shake with cold. I see thick green vegetation away to my left on the beach.

"Water." I go across and sure enough, there is a small stream, I drink deeply and then wash the sand out of my wounds. Then I remember that salt is supposed to be good for cuts so I splash some sea water onto them.

"Shit!" That really hurts. I am barefooted and my hands are bleeding so I tear off some shreds from my suit and tie them around my feet and hands, making some very basic footwear and gloves. Next on my list is some warmth, yeah I am hungry but that is not going to kill me, hypothermia will. I think about a fire, will it put me in danger? But then I decide that I will die without one so I set too. I don't recognise any of the plants, though they all look familiar - ish. I find a tree that has a silvery bark, which you can pull off, almost like paper, it will make good kindling. I find a stringy looking green plant and make some reasonable strength rope, then a bit of soft wood, a bit of hardwood and young sampling.

I am finding it difficult to concentrate, I keep fading in and out of focus; the pain in my head is getting worse. It takes a while, but I setup up the scout's trick of rubbing two bits of wood together, but with the benefit of a bow driving them. It's hard work and takes a long time, but after a couple of hours, I have smouldering embers. I lift them in my hands and blow, slowly at first, then harder, until a bright orange flame springs up. I quickly pile on some of the bark, then twigs and quickly I have a roaring fire. Not soon enough either, I have blue hands and I am starting to shake uncontrollably. I pile on some more wood and build a log wall behind the fire to reflect the heat at me, after about half an hour I am feeling warm and ready for some food. The pain in my head is getting progressively worse, I am starting to worry that I won't be functioning soon. I scavenge around and find all sorts of berries and roots, but I have no idea whether I can eat any of them. I can't afford to get ill, but I gather them anyway, I might get desperate enough to eat them. Just as I am starting to get depressed I see some sort of bird, I am sure that I can eat that. I pick up a large rock and wait, it seems to be a ground bird and walks around for a while until coming to within throwing range. I weigh the stone in my hand for the 200th time and let loose, boom, it hits the bird. It doesn't kill it, but stuns it enough for me to be on top of it and ringing its neck. Twenty minutes later and it's cleaned and skewered and turning over my fire. Life is good – apart for the pain in my head.

I turn the bird over on its skewer and say out loud.

"Wouldn't Wolf be proud of me?"

But then I think; "Who the hell is Wolf." I honestly can't quite form a picture of Wolf nor for that matter anything else. This is the first time I get to sit and think about what's going in. I realise, somewhat shaken that I am struggling with current events. I know that I am Major Lance, I can name my friends, regimental officers, everything, but I have no idea of where I am or what I am doing and just as importantly how I got here. Absent mindedly I wonder if this is another Marine Escape and Evade test where they have disorientated me with a drug; or maybe it's that thing caused by diving, after all, I know that I was in the water. I remember from my diving course that you can start acting like your drunk from nitrogen poisoning. Either way, I will do what I can to make myself comfortable and wait for a rescue. The meat is done and just as I start to pull the meat off the bone I hear a noise.

I look up and there's a group of five men, no more than 10 paces away. My first thought is that they are a lot closer than I should have let them get, maybe this knock on my head is dulling my senses. They are dark and short, but lean looking. Each is naked except for a Tartan dress, they have long hair cut squarely around their faces and stunning geometric tattoos in dark blue on their tanned bodies. But what really worries me is that they have spears or at least sticks with flint ends. They stand there in neutral positions, neither threatening nor passive.

I stand, but as I do, the blood rushes out of my head and I feel very faint and nauseous – I am being to lose it.

I look at the men. My vision is blurry, but I am sure the one in the middle is closer by two paces. I have a weird feeling of being very drunk and the world is slowly spinning. I try to re-focus on the men, again their leader is two paces closer. My brain is playing tricks on me, each time I sway and fight for consciousness, I look at the man. Each time he is closer, but I haven't seen him move.

For the first time, I notice he is carrying a club. He is now within arms-reach. He smiles at me and like the last drunk at the bar I smile back dumbly.

Thud……..

The Author

Andy Bex grew up in Sheffield at a time when his friends formed famous pop groups, become artists or business moguls. He therefore naturally assumed that he could write a novel. Andy has also been steadily preparing for Armageddon and holds a British army commission, black belt in Ju Jitsu and is a champion fencer – Zombies beware!